Praise for the writing of J. L. Langley

The Tin Star

"JL Langley's *The Tin Star* is ... read for anyone who loves non-traditional/homo-erotic/gay stories. This fabulous tale will make your eyes tear at its poignancy and laughter will regularly escape from you throughout. I can't wait for more from JL Langley!"

-- Elizabeth, *Euro-Reviews*

"Ms. Langley should be commended for writing not only a beautiful story, but one that has huge social ramifications. This book is a Recommended Read!"

-- Teresa, *Fallen Angel Reviews*

The Broken H

"From the first sentences of *The Broken H* I lost sight of the fact that I was reading a novel, and simply fell into the story as if I was watching it happen in front of me."

-- *Two Lips Reviews*

"*The Broken H* is a deliciously satisfying story with a pair of unforgettable heroes. Funny, sexy and sweet, J.L. Langley has crafted an excellent tale that I highly recommend."

-- Isabelle Spencer, *Romance Reviews Today*

LooseId®

ISBN 10: 1-59632-048-6
ISBN 13: 978-1-59632-048-2
THE BROKEN H
Copyright © 2007 J L Langley
Originally released in e-book format in September 2006

Cover Art by April Martinez

Printed in the U.S.A. by
Lightning Source, Inc.
1246 Heil Quaker Blvd
La Vergne TN 37086
www.lightningsource.com

THE BROKEN H

J. L. Langley

Dedication

To Olivia Wong -- What a team!!! MWAH! Thanks also to my wonderful critique group; Jet Mykles for her great input; April Martinez for her work on the cover; and, as always my love, my soul mate, Andre.

Chapter One

Damned broken rubber band. Shane Cortez batted the stray black hair out of his face and once again considered rolling up the windows and turning on the A/C of the battered old ranch truck, but it was too nice outside. He was definitely going to have to get some of those elastic ponytail holders that women and girls used. His hair was just too darned thick. This rubber band was the third one he'd snapped this week.

He tucked the long and heavy strands behind the earpiece of his sunglasses again, then wound the windows up half way, hoping that it would help keep his hair from flying into his eyes and yet maintain the cool temperature. He was almost home, surely he could deal with both that long. Then he could rebraid his hair before he unloaded the supplies. If he could find a damned rubber band that is.

Shane drove up the Broken H's drive and pulled to the rear of the house, slipping between his personal truck and the back fence of the big white colonial ranch house. He had barely gotten the truck in park before he saw Kaitlyn Hunter run toward him, her gray-streaked red hair flying wildly behind her.

His stomach knotted up with dread. Although the lady was still pretty lively for her age -- her husband, Ted, liked to tease that it was the Irish in her -- Shane could remember seeing that mane of red hair unbound only once in the entire twenty-six years he'd work on the Broken H: the morning the Hunters' son, Gray, had been shot in the line of duty while on a drug raid with the rest of the San Antonio SWAT team.

Oh, God! Grayson. Shane sucked in a breath, trying his best to keep nausea at bay even as he quickly opened the door and jumped out of the truck. "What is it Kaitlyn? What's wrong?"

She came to a stop only a few feet from him, her petite body shaking. "Shane, hurry! It's Ted! I think he's having a heart attack!"

Damn, damn, damn! Shane sprinted toward the ranch house, his heart pounding. Ted couldn't be dying. He couldn't! Hell, the man was only in his early sixties and had always been in reasonably good health. "Kaitlyn, did you call Grayson?"

"Oh, no! I didn't think about it. I was about to get my car when you pulled up, Shane." Kaitlyn could barely get the words out, her voice wavering.

Shane reached the kitchen and stopped dead in his tracks.

Ted was sitting at the kitchen table, his head resting on his arms. His gray hair fell into his eyes as his head popped up. Although he was pale and his face was a little pinched, he wasn't the dying, thrashing heap Shane's horrible imagination had conjured.

"Ted?" Shane frowned and rushed forward to put a hand on the older man's shoulder.

"Shane. Did you get everything we needed from the feed store?" Ted's voice was just a little strained.

He nodded. "Are you okay? Kaitlyn said you aren't feeling too well."

"Well, son, Katy's right. I've got to say I've been better. You think you can drive me up to the hospital?"

"Absolutely." Shane grabbed Ted under an arm and helped him to stand. The fact that he was willing to go to the hospital without being dragged kicking and screaming said more than anything how bad Ted must be feeling.

He all but carried the man out to Shane's newer Chevy, about three yards away from the beat up blue ranch truck. As he settled Ted and Kaitlyn in the back of the silver quad cab and got behind the wheel, he calculated how close the nearest hospital was. He wasn't ready to lose his...well, Ted was like a father to him. The older man and Kaitlyn had taken Shane in when he was sixteen; they were his family. Speaking of which...

As he left the driveway, Shane dug through his center console, hoping that was where he'd left his cell phone. He handed it to Kaitlyn with a brief word about calling her son, then quickly glanced back at Ted. Incredibly, Ted was the most calm among the three of them.

Kaitlyn's small hand was hot and not quite steady as she took the phone from Shane. After a few seconds, she let out a distressed sound. "Darn it, Shane, I can't work this thing! Is there a trick to it?"

Shane held out his hand again. "Let me see it. I'll dial Gray and you can talk to him." The phone touched his palm but was snatched away before he could close his fingers around it.

"Nonsense, Katy. Darlin', the boy is driving. He can't be dialing a phone. I'll do it."

Shane grinned, feeling much better about the situation. If Ted could still remain calm and take charge, he must not be as bad off as they feared.

The drive to the hospital was long and intense, but they finally made it. The emergency room doctor admitted Ted and immediately started running tests. Now all there was to do was wait. He hated waiting.

Kaitlyn had gone into the examining room with her husband and left Shane to make the appropriate calls and fill out the admissions paperwork. Ted had left a message with one of Gray's deputies, but Shane hadn't seen hide nor hair of the man himself. At one point during the interminable wait, Kaitlyn came to tell him that Ted had indeed had a heart attack, but she knew very little else. The doctors were still checking him out.

Shane had already called the Broken H to let the ranch hands know what was going on as well as told them to unload the truck. He'd looked out the window a couple of times and flipped through a magazine. He was doing anything he could think of to pass the time without worrying, but nothing was helping much. He was about to rise and search for a cup of coffee when a hand touched his shoulder.

"Shane?"

He looked up into eyes the color of freshly cut grass and swallowed the lump in his throat. Why, after all these years, did the man still affect him this way? He stood and extended his hand, hoping like hell that the tremble of his fingers would be passed off as nerves from Ted being in the hospital.

"Hello, Grayson."

It was a stupid thing, and ridiculous to say the least, considering his father was in the hospital, possibly dying, but the first thing Gray noticed was that Shane's long black hair was down. He wished he could run his fingers through that glorious mane and erase the haunted look from Shane's regal face. The man looked like the pictures of Native Americans in history books after they'd been forced onto reservations, defeated and hurt, but still proud.

Shane tugged on his hand. *Damn!* He hadn't even realized he still had hold of the man. What was it about Shane that always had him making a complete and utter ass of himself?

Gray cleared his throat and sat down next to the one Shane had vacated, trying to regain his composure. Being this close to Shane was always disorienting, but receiving a message that his father was in the hospital with a suspected heart attack wasn't helping his nerves either. "Have you heard anything about Dad's condition? Is he going to be all right?"

Shane shrugged and sat down beside him. "Your mother told me the doctor said he did have a heart attack, but she didn't know much more than that. They are still doing tests on him."

Gray nodded, not sure what to say. He hadn't been the world's greatest son by any stretch of the imagination, but he loved his dad. "I need to get out to the Broken H more."

"Sad that it takes something like this to make you realize it."

Gray wasn't sure Shane meant to censure him, but it was there in his voice all the same. "What the fuck is that supposed to mean?"

Shane raised an arrogant brow.

Smug bastard!

"Do you really want to argue right now, Grayson?"

"You started it, Cortez!" *Un-fucking-believable.* It wasn't like he didn't already feel guilty about not visiting his folks as much as he should, but now the reason he stayed away was giving him shit about it.

Shane sighed and ran his hands down his tanned face. "Look, you're right. I'm sorry. I'm worried about your dad."

What? And Gray wasn't? He wanted to slug Shane, but he didn't. He'd grown up with the man and knew that Shane did genuinely care for the older Hunters. Besides, Gray might be aggravated, but he wasn't going to let Shane see it. Of course, the man was always under his skin, so it was really moot. Gray sighed and rested his head in his hands, trying to relax. "I'm worried, too. I might not go out to the ranch that often, but he's still my dad."

"Shane? Oh! Gray!"

Gray looked up to see his mom jog toward them, smiling. He stood up and held his arms wide. "Hi, Mom. How is he?"

She squeezed him tight, then cupped a hand behind his neck, pulling him down to kiss his cheek. "First they're going to do an angiogram to see how bad the damage to the heart's blood vessels are. Then they'll know if he needs bypass surgery. If it's not too bad, they can fix it when they do the angioplasty rather than doing the bypass. They put these little stents in there to open up the blood vessels."

Oh, God! He knew it sounded scarier than it probably was, but he couldn't help his initial shocked reaction.

Shane looked as unshakable as always, and it annoyed the piss out of him. The man was a freaking rock. *Wait! Was that a bit of moisture in his eyes?* Shane glanced at him, face unreadable, and blinked.

"It's really not that big a deal nowadays, Grayson. He'll be fine."

"Yeah, I know." He looked back at his mother. "When are they going to do the procedure?"

"The doctor is going to take him back in in about two hours. Do you boys want to see him before they start prepping him? The nurse said it would be okay, but just for a few minutes."

Gray grabbed her hand, patting it, then tugged her to get her moving. "Of course we do, Mom."

When they walked in to the patient room, his dad smiled. God, he looked like hell. Gray tried his best to smile back and went to the side of the bed. Taking his father's hand, he squeezed it before letting go. "Hey, Pop."

"Hey, kiddo." Ted glanced to Gray's other side and spotted Shane, dipping his head in greeting. "Shane."

"Ted." Shane inclined his chin slightly, his face harder than ever.

"Since I've got both you boys here, "he grabbed Gray's hand, then Shane's, "I want y'all to keep the Broken H going. I want the two of you...both my boys --"

"Dad, you aren't dying, so knock it off."

Shane frowned at him. "Let the man talk, Grayson."

Oh, good lord! Didn't it bother Shane to have the old man talking like he was about to die? It sure as hell did him. Gray heaved a large sigh and shut his mouth before he said something he'd regret.

Ted gripped their hands. "Now, listen up. I'm not expecting to die, son. But I want to make sure things are taken care of in case something should happen. Gray --"

"Dad?"

"I want you to help out Shane the next couple of weeks. Now, I know you have responsibility as sheriff, but I'd like you to make time if Shane needs you."

Gray nodded. He'd already cleared his schedule, but he was hoping like hell that Shane didn't need him. Working with Shane, seeing him all day, every day, would likely kill him, even if it were for just a week or two. Still, he'd be there to lend a hand if he had to. Hell, worrying about it was probably all for naught since Shane ran the Broken H by himself anyway. The man had pretty much taken over all the managerial stuff, including paying bills and making the ranch decisions, years ago while his father just managed a few things here and there.

"I will, Dad. I've already taken a few days off. My deputies can handle things by themselves for a while."

Ted smiled. "Good, good." He squeezed their hands again. "And you will both take care of Katy?"

Gray took a deep breath. He hated the doom and gloom and what if's, especially in this situation with regard to someone he loved.

Shane glanced at him across the bed. There was a slight arch of one of those proud brows. Then the man looked back at his dad. "Of course, we will, Ted. But you are going to be out in no time and will be able to do that yourself."

"I sure hope so, Shane."

"Shane's right, Dad. I bet you'll be home within a week."

The nurse stepped inside the doorway. "All right, gentlemen. I'm going to have to run you out of here. We have to get Mr. Hunter ready." She shooed them toward the door. "Mrs. Hunter, you can stay for a few more minutes."

"See you, Dad. Love you." Gray bent and kissed his father's cheek.

The old man patted him on the shoulder. "Love you, too, Gray."

Shane looked past Gray. "I'm going to go grab a bite to eat, Kaitlyn. You want anything?"

"No, honey, I'm good. You go and take Gray with you. And make him eat something, Shane. That way I'll know he got at least one good meal today."

Shane looked back at Ted, his face unreadable, or it would have been to most people, but Gray knew the man. He knew that slight head dip said everything Shane wouldn't say aloud, that he loved Gray's dad, too. "Ted."

Apparently, his dad realized it as well. He chuckled and reached out a hand to Shane. When Shane took it, Ted pulled him close and patted his shoulder, just as he'd done to Gray. "Love you, too, boy! Now y'all get. Eat something good for me, too, because I have a feeling they are going to tell me I have to watch my diet after this."

Gray heard the nurse chuckle as they left.

"You better believe it, Mr. Hunter."

He and Shane got back into the waiting area before Shane dropped a bomb on him. "I probably will need you to help out next week. I had to let one of the hands go and another one is out on vacation."

Gray closed his eyes for a few seconds, then opened them and nodded. *Well, son of a bitch!* Didn't that just figure?

Chapter Two

Shane was pretty sure Gray hadn't wanted to go eat with him, but he'd agreed anyhow. Now the other man sat quietly in the truck next to him, staring out the side window with his tan cowboy hat pulled low over his eyes. What had happened to the easy camaraderie they'd had between them?

Once upon a time there was no one Shane had felt more comfortable with, not even Ted and Kaitlyn, than Gray. He had been Shane's shadow up until Gray was almost eighteen. Then, shortly after, Gray had up and taken off to ride the rodeo circuit. Oh man, had that scared the crap out of Shane. Kaitlyn and Ted, too, for that matter. But Shane also had been proud. Gray had really made a name for himself in bull riding -- he could have gone on to the pro circuit if he'd wanted to -- instead the boy had put himself through college with his winnings, then joined the San Antonio Police Department. After a short career with the SWAT team, Gray had come back home and run for sheriff; he had been the youngest man to be voted in as sheriff in the history of their county.

Shane turned the truck into the diner parking lot, found a spot and paused before cutting the engine. "This okay? Or do you want something else?"

Gray opened the door and got out. "No, this is fine." He shut the door and started for the entrance.

Shane sighed, switched off the ignition and joined him. Gray's attitude sucked and had done so since he'd left home eleven years ago. But damn if his ass didn't look good in those khaki uniform pants as he stormed across the lot. Shane groaned and shook his head as he followed that fine ass inside the diner.

Once they were seated in a booth, a waitress took their order and brought iced teas. Through it all, Gray hardly said a word. He wouldn't even look at Shane.

Shane had had enough. He had no idea why the man was so hostile toward him, but it ate at him and they were going to talk about this. Gray was too important to him. He always had been.

What Shane really wanted...well, it didn't matter what he wanted. Gray might not be a kid anymore, but he was still too young for Shane. And Gray deserved better than Shane, but, damn it, they were not going to continue this way! He missed the old Gray; whatever it was that was bothering the man was also keeping him away from the Broken H -- away from his parents and away from Shane.

He had just opened his mouth to question Gray, when Sherry Ann, the Hunters' neighbor's teenaged daughter, slid into the seat beside him. Her blond ponytail almost hit him in the face as she scooted close. *Damn! Not again!* The girl practically pounced on him every time she saw him.

"Hey, there, Shane! What brings you into town?" She pursed her lips a little and pressed her arms to her sides, causing her breasts to appear as they might spill out of the low-cut blue blouse at any minute.

"Family emergency, Sherry Ann." He scooted closer to the wall and gave her a look he hoped conveyed that he wanted her to go away.

She ignored it and slid in closer to him. "Nothing too bad, I hope." Bold as you please, she reached out and wound her finger around a strand of his hair, playing with it. "I've never seen your hair down. You should wear it like this more often. It's really sexy." The minx actually batted her lashes at him. "If you're not doing anything Saturday, I'd love to repay you for saving me the other day."

Good Lord, the girl had nerve! Shane managed not to groan. Since Sherry Ann had hit puberty, she'd been coming on to him and trying to seduce him, but in the past few months, it seemed as though she'd doubled her efforts. She blatantly made a pass at him every time she saw him, regardless of how many times he refused her.

Shane brushed his hair over his shoulder, effectively removing the strands from her fingers, wished once again that he had something to pull it back with and squeezed toward the wall. "Sherry Ann, I've told you time and again, I'm way too old for you."

Gray cleared his throat. Was he glaring at the girl? No, more than likely he was just reminding her of her manners.

She looked up at him, startled. "Oh, hi there, Sheriff Hunter."

Gray tipped his head, "Sherry Ann." Apparently, it reminded him of his own manners. He seemed to realize that his cowboy hat was still on his head, pulled it off, and set it on the seat next to him, then ran a hand through his short dark-brown hair. "Shane saved you?"

She looked back at Shane, grabbing his hair again. "Yup. I ran my car into a ditch, but Shane rescued me. He drove me so I didn't have to walk the whole rest of the way home."

It was all Shane could do to keep from rolling his eyes. She had only been a mile away from her home. The walk wouldn't have killed her. What was it going to take to make the girl understand he didn't want her? He'd flat out told her he wasn't interested...several times.

Gray's bright green eyes narrowed on Shane, then he looked back at Sherry Ann. Did Gray glare at her again? Shane jerked his hair out of her hand, not caring how it appeared. *Enough is enough!*

Gray's eyes widened and met his; a smile quirked at the corner of his lips before he leaned forward toward the girl. "Darlin', I hate to be rude and run you off, but I have some business to discuss with Shane."

She leaned her arms on the table, giving Gray her undivided attention -- and exposed her cleavage some more. "Oh! Police business? What did Shane do?"

Shane groaned aloud. "Shane didn't do anything!" He winced. *Good Lord!* Not only had that come out rather snappish, but he'd actually referred to himself in the third person.

Gray laughed, showing off the dimple in his left cheek. "He really didn't do anything, but I really do need to talk to him privately, if you don't mind."

She sighed dramatically. "Well, okay. Think about this weekend, all right, Shane?" She kissed his cheek and got up.

Before Shane complain about her forwardness and tell her that he wasn't going to see her this weekend -- or any other weekend -- she left them.

"What in hell was that about?"

He looked up into Gray's grinning face. God, how long had it been since he'd seen Gray smile like that? The handsome youth had grown into an even more handsome man. Shane beamed back at him, then sobered. "The girl is a nuisance. She keeps propositioning me. No matter how often and how many ways I turn her down, damn it, she just doesn't take no for an answer. I swear it seems like I bump into her everywhere. She calls me at the ranch and even my cell phone the other day."

Gray stopped smiling. "She's stalking you?"

What? Stalking? Shane blinked. "Don't be ridiculous, she's just a kid. She might be a pain in the ass, but she's harmless. She just needs a good spanking." Not that Shane was going to volunteer to give it to her. No doubt the hussy would probably enjoy that. "Actually, I feel sorry for her. It's too bad her mom died so young; I don't think her daddy gives her any attention. He buys her affection with fancy clothes and things, and he just got her that car. The kid is clearly starved for attention."

Gray's brows pulled together. "I don't know, Shane. She's got to be around seventeen now, not much of a kid anymore. If you've told her no and she keeps bugging you...that's not right. You're sure you've made it clear to her?"

"Is telling her, 'Sherry Ann, I'm too old for you. You need to stop this flirting, because I'm not going to go out with you' clear?"

"Yeah, that's pretty obvious." Those beautiful lips frowned some more, turning down at the corners. "And she continues to pester you." It wasn't really a question, but Shane nodded anyway.

Gray shook his head. "Shane, that sounds like some pretty obsessive behavior. It needs to be stopped."

"I'm more concerned that the kid is going to pull that shit with some other man and get herself into something she can't handle. I've been thinking seriously about getting your mother to have a talk with her. The only reason I haven't done so myself is that coming from me, she might take it as encouragement."

Gray took a sip of his tea, still grim. He set his glass back down. "Maybe you should go talk to her father."

Shane snorted. "Hell, the man would probably try to marry her off to me just to get her out of his hair. He doesn't really care what the kid does as long as she doesn't bother him."

Gray looked him in the eye. "Seriously, Chief, you should do something about it. It *is* stalking."

Shane blinked, dumbfounded. All thoughts of Sherry Ann flew from his mind; Gray hadn't called him "Chief" in years. God, he'd missed that! As always, if it had come from anyone else, Shane would have been pissed as hell, but Gray didn't mean it as an insult; he never had. It was a term of respect from a four-year-old Gray and, later, a term of endearment. The boy had walked right up to Shane, those green eyes peering up at him in awe, and asked, "Are you a war chief or a peace chief? Can I be a brave? Will you teach me how?"

"What's the matter?" Gray's head cocked a little.

Shane broke away from his reverie. "Nothing."

They shared an awkward moment, both staring at the other, then Gray's eyes twinkled. "You know, speaking of marriage, why haven't you found a nice girl and settled down?"

Shane chuckled, relieved to not only have the silence broken, but to have Gray teasing him. "Why haven't you? Heck, kill two birds with one stone. You could solve my problem and get yourself a girl by asking Sherry Ann out. She's much closer to your age than mine."

Gray leaned forward, eyes suddenly serious. "Yeah, but I think we both know she's not my type...on account of the fact that she doesn't have a dick. Or had you forgotten?"

Chapter Three

It was just after midnight by the time Gray made it to his parents' place. After finding out that his dad would be undergoing a double bypass in the morning, Gray had called his office to let everyone know where they could reach him. Then he'd gone to the house he'd rented outside in town, changed out of his uniform into jeans and a black T-shirt, packed some clothes and headed out to the ranch. His mother had decided to stay at the hospital. So here he was, pulling through the front gate under the wrought iron arch that read, "The Broken H."

The dirt and gravel drive was long and wound around to the back of the main ranch house, past the gleaming white columns in front that were lit with up lights; however, the porch light was off. Gray pulled around back, noting that the back porch light was off as well. Damn, he'd loved this place as a kid. Too bad this didn't feel like home anymore. He hadn't been comfortable here since that day by the stock tank twelve years ago. The day his world had changed.

Gray snorted and parked his truck. It was a long time ago. He hardly ever thought about it nowadays. Okay, that was a lie; he thought about that day every time he saw Shane, every time he went fishing -- which he never did anymore -- or whenever the Broken H was mentioned. It really was time to get over it. After all, Shane hadn't blinked an eye when Gray reminded him that he was gay. He thought that was promising. Maybe he and Shane could build some semblance of the friendship they had had back then. Maybe Shane had grown to accept Gray's sexual orientation. He hoped so.

Gray grabbed his duffle bag from the passenger side of his truck and shut the door. Even though the lights were off at the big house, the front porch light was on at Shane's three-bedroom cottage, where the foreman traditionally lived. Should he go there, let Shane know that he was here? Damn, he wanted to...and that irritated the piss out of him. Why did Shane still matter so much to him? Why was seeing if they could at least be friends again such a big deal? Shane had made his feelings pretty apparent long ago, but what about today? They'd actually gotten along today.

"Well, fuck!" Gray slung his bag over his shoulder and headed to the foreman's cottage. Maybe if he got it over with and Shane told him to fuck off, he could then get his head out of the clouds. Or maybe he was just an idiot!

He stepped up on the porch and knocked at the door. What a far cry from when he was a kid: he'd have just walked in back then.

"It's open!" Shane's bellow was muffled.

Gray turned the knob and entered the living room. It looked just the same as he remembered: same hardwood floor, same wood paneling on the walls, same old brown leather furniture. The mantle above the stone fireplace had a few new pictures, but other than that, nothing much appeared to have changed. Gray had always liked this room with all the wood; it always felt homey, lived in, rustic and manly. It was a comfortable room.

He noticed Shane had almost filled up the bookshelves by the fireplace. The man had always loved to read, but rarely did so back when Gray had lived on the Broken H. There had always been so much to do. More than once, Shane had set aside a book to take him riding, or fishing, or hunting or whatever Gray had wanted to do.

"Grayson? Is that you?"

"Yeah. Where are you?"

"Kitchen."

Gray dropped his duffle by the couch and crossed the room to the open dining room and on into the kitchen. He looked around, observing that the kitchen appliances and cabinets had been updated -- stainless steel and dark oak -- then his gaze landed on Shane -- or rather Shane's ass.

His fantasy man was on his knees and one hand. His other hand reached between the refrigerator and a cabinet. His face was turned away from Gray and his long hair cascaded over a shoulder to puddle on the floor. Other than a pair of red plaid sleep pants, he wore nothing else. A long line of tan, sleekly muscled back provided a showcase above that nice plaid-encased ass. Even the man's damned feet were sexy!

Gray bit back a groan and moved closer so he could be seen.

Shane's handsome face was mashed up against the cabinet. His big brown eyes met Gray's and his eyebrows were pinched together in concentration.

"What are you doing?"

Shane sighed loudly. "I swear by God and all that is holy it's a fucking conspiracy! Rubber bands are out to get me!"

He said it with such conviction that Gray burst out laughing. He peered down into the three-inch space between the fridge and the cabinet. A little more than a finger's width from Shane's outstretched hand was the recalcitrant rubber band. "Uh, Chief? I really hate to ask, but did you consider maybe getting a broom or something with a long handle --"

Shane groaned and got up. "Smart ass!" He went to the pantry, long hair covering his sinewy back and falling just above that magnificent ass, and pulled a broom out, then pointed a finger at Gray, "Don't you dare laugh! It's been a long day; my brain is tired." He fished out the offending conspirator and replaced the broom, then leaned against the cabinet and began to braid his hair. "Have you been to the big house yet?"

"Nope. I saw your light on and thought I'd let you know I was here so you didn't shoot me for trespassing."

Shane rolled his eyes. "I was expecting you. Remind me tomorrow to look in your dad's office for some more rubber bands. This is my last one; the damned thing escaped by flying right out of my hand." He finished the braid and wrapped the band around it once, twice, three times, then was done.

Gray stared; he couldn't help it. And to make matters worse, he was getting hard.

To say that Shane had a beautiful body was an understatement. The man was gorgeous. He was about as tall as Gray -- six foot or so -- but where Gray was more heavily muscled, Shane had the body of an athlete or, as Gray used to think, an Indian warrior. His chest would look so right with a bear claw painted on it, or with a bone breastplate worn over it...

Shane caught his gaze. An eyebrow lifted. Then in a soft, husky voice he said, "Come here."

Gray blinked, caught off guard. "Huh?"

Shane crossed his arms over his chest, and continued to lean against the cabinet. His face was unreadable. "I said, come here."

Gray moved slowly. His feet felt like they weighed a ton. What did Shane want? When he got about two feet away, Shane pushed away from the cabinet and closed the space between them. Gray could have sworn he felt butterflies in his stomach.

He was afraid to breathe, afraid Shane would move away -- afraid that he wouldn't. What was he to do? He stood there watching, waiting, and swallowed down the lump in his throat. Gray had long since memorized every inch of the face before him, those high cheek bones, the long straight nose and the thick black lashes covering those beautiful brown eyes, but damned if his cock didn't harden completely at seeing them this close. Shane's dark eyes gazed back for several seconds. Then his sensual lips turned up so slightly that if Gray hadn't been staring at his mouth, he'd have missed it.

Shane reached behind Gray's neck, pulled him forward...and kissed him.

Gray's brain shorted out. The butterflies in his gut started doing donuts and popping wheelies and all he could do was stand there...frozen. What the hell was happening? Shane didn't like him that way. Hell, more to the point, Shane wasn't gay. He'd discovered that the hard way when Shane had rejected him all those years ago.

But now the older man smiled against his lips and moved back slightly. His thumb rubbed back and forth on Gray's neck. "You always did think too much. Just stop it and open your mouth."

"I --"

Shane's lips slanted over his; his tongue pushed deeply inside. He tenderly traced Gray's teeth and mouth with his tongue, caressing and exploring all at once.

Gray forgot how to breathe, he might have even whimpered when Shane's other hand came to his waist, tugging him flush against that lean body; he could feel Shane's erection against his own.

He lost it, it was his dream come to life -- not just any dream, but one he had had all too frequently throughout the years -- and a wet one at that. Until Shane came to his senses and ceased the delicious embrace, he was going to enjoy it. A little voice in the back of his head whispered, *Bad idea, Gray. Think about the consequences,* but he didn't care. He'd probably never get the chance again.

Tightly wrapping his arms around Shane, he caressed that strong, smooth back, even as his tongue returned the attention it received. He tried to go slow, savor it, remember every detail, but damned if Shane didn't derail him. Hands wandered up under his shirt, caressed his back, then moved around to his chest, plucking at his erect nipples. A tingle ran up Gray's spine, making him shiver in delight.

Finally, Shane broke their kiss, flipping Gray's shirt over his head and dropping it to the floor. A finger ran down Gray's torso, starting between his smooth pecs and ending at his navel. Shane dipped that meandering digit inside the hollow, then followed the trail of hair, starting below his navel, until he hit the top of the low waistband of Gray's jeans.

Gray watched Shane watch him, those brown eyes practically scorching his body as they followed the line down. Then, before Gray even realized what he was about, Shane bent over and traced the same path with his tongue.

He couldn't breathe, his breath hitched in his throat and refused to leave. Was this really happening? "Shane..."

"Relax." Shane rose and kissed him again, this time charting a moist course and nipping along his neck and shoulder, leaving goose bumps in his wake. When he got to Gray's collarbone, he reached down and unfastened Gray's jeans.

Oh, God! Gray's balls pulled tighter, his cock jerking in anticipation. When that tanned, callused hand slipped inside and found his prick, his hips pushed forward, practically begging. Shane squeezed and rubbed through the thin cotton of his boxers. His prick started to leak. Shane moaned and squeezed again as his mouth surrounded Gray's nipple.

"Fuck!" He pulled Shane closer, cradling his head against his chest with one hand, stroking his back with the other. If he was only going to get to do this once, he was going to seize the opportunity and finally play with that glorious and silken black mane. He snatched the end of Shane's braid, pulled the band off and unraveled it. How many times had he dreamed of combing his fingers through it? Lifting several strands, he let them fall again.

Shane sighed softly and moved his mouth down Gray's chest. When he reached Gray's dick, he hooked his thumbs through the waistband of the jeans and pushed them and Gray's boxers down in one quick motion.

Gray's prick bobbed free, standing straight up, feeling unbelievably sensitive in the cool air. He was so fucking hard he ached. He wanted Shane's mouth, his hands, something...anything on his cock. "Holy shit!"

Shane's tongue flicked over the tip, then engulfed his dick in the moist heat of his mouth. Gray groaned, fingers tightening in the thick black hair. Shane groaned too, then stood up, making Gray cry out at the loss of those beautiful lips.

"Bedroom, Grayson." Shane leaned forward and brushed a quick kiss against him. "Now."

Gray's mind protested, telling him to make a break for it, to get out while he could before he did something they'd both probably regret. His cock had other ideas, it told him to keep his mouth shut and get his ass in the bedroom. Naturally, his cock won the argument.

He sat down on the end of Shane's big mahogany four-poster and yanked off his sneakers, then his socks. By the time he was completely nude, Shane was with him again. The other man walked right up to him, standing between his spread legs. Those warm brown eyes looked up and down.

"Very nice." Shane leaned forward, resting his hands on Gray's shoulders and flicked his tongue across Gray's lips.

He melted, opened right up and let Shane in. His hands encircled the other man's taut waist, fingers inching the waistband down. The kissing was great, but he was dying to get a hold of Shane's cock. He leaned back, separating their mouths, to untie the drawstring and pulled the pants the rest of the way off. *Oh, God, yes!*

Shane's prick came free. For some strange reason Gray had always thought Shane would be uncut, but he was glad to see that he was wrong; he liked the look of a circumcised prick much better. It was long, had a deep red tint to it as well as a really pronounced vein down its length. The head was nice and thick. His mouth watered just staring at it. Wondering about how Shane would taste was one of the things that had driven him crazy for years. Now he enveloped the base of that fat prick with his hand, moved it forward, and closed his lips around it.

He loved sucking cock; it had always been one of his favorite things to do and he was damned good at it. But the fact that it was Shane's dick made it even more enjoyable. He slid all the way down, taking the wide shaft deep into his mouth, then back up. On the next descent, he swallowed as the head lodged in the back of his throat.

Shane's fingers flexed on his shoulders and hoarse, sexy groan filled the air. He reached down and tipped Gray's chin up, those brown eyes half lidded and filled with lust. "Damn, you look pretty with your lips wrapped around my dick, but I don't want you to do this right now. Scoot up on the bed, Grayson."

Gray thought about arguing, but no way was he going to give Shane a reason to call a halt to their fun. He didn't know what had gotten into the man, but he wasn't about to look a gift horse in the mouth, so to speak. He wanted him too badly and was certain he'd only have the memory of this to last him forever, so he gave the sweet prick one last good suck and pulled away.

"Oh, damn, you're good at that." Shane tapped Gray's leg and flipped his own chin toward the headboard. "Come on, up in the middle of the bed."

Gray slid back as he was told and watched as Shane crawled up on the bed after him. Damn, the man was beautiful! He moved so gracefully, always had, but watching him move across the bed naked was something else. Shane looked like a tiger stalking his prey and Gray's belly tensed from the sight. His lover's long dark hair parted on each side of his head and trailed over Gray's limbs, tickling in a sensual way. Gray's cock leaked more fluid. Fuck, he wanted Shane so bad!

Shane reached Gray's cock and stopped, still on his hands and knees, his hair now brushing Gray's hips. He sat up enough to pull his hair back over his shoulder, out of his face, then he held Gray's gaze and slowly licked the drops off the Gray's dick. "Mmmm…"

Gray's eyes squeezed shut and his back arched off the bed. "Oh, fucking shit, Shane!"

Shane's hand pushed on his stomach. "Lie down and relax, love."

Yeah, right. Relaxing was a little hard to do when the man of your dreams -- *Oh, God!*

Shane's hot mouth surrounded his dick. Gray's eyes flew open and his neck lifted; he *had* to see. Shane worked his cock in and out, going deeper every time, those tanned cheeks hollowing out when he came up. His hand gripped the base of Gray's prick and moved in tandem with Shane's lips, pumping up and down. It was the hottest thing Gray had ever seen in his life. Hell, it was the hottest thing he'd ever *felt* in his life. His balls pulled tight. He was so damned close to coming, it was almost funny. He normally had great stamina and good staying power, but Shane had him so wired he was ready to blow in less than five minutes. He moaned, and it sounded like a whimper.

It briefly crossed his mind that Shane seemed to know what he was doing, but then he couldn't think anymore, only feel; he dropped his head back and closed his eyes again, concentrated hard on not coming. It wasn't working; it felt beyond incredible and he *knew* it was Shane. It was all too much. "Shane... Stop!"

Cool air hit his wet prick as that wonderful mouth withdrew. The bed shifted.

"Close?"

Gray nodded, then lifted his lids. *Oh, shit!* Shane's lips were red and swollen from sucking him. He'd also sat up and that gorgeous hair was falling over his shoulders and down his chest again. His lover's abs flexed slightly as he breathed and his prick was still erect, arching up toward his dark belly. It was --

"...top drawer of the nightstand." Shane kissed the inside of his thigh and settled back on his feet.

Gray had totally zoned; he had no idea what Shane was saying. What was in the top drawer?

Shane grinned at him, knowingly. "There you go again, thinking too much. There are condoms and lube in the top drawer. Get them, Grayson."

Lube? Condoms? Gray blinked. Yeah, he could do that. He scrambled up the bed and opened the drawer. Sure enough, there was a tube of KY and several foil packages. He tore one off the row, grabbed the lube and shut the drawer. Somewhere in the back of his mind a little voice was once again asking why Shane was doing this. Shane wasn't gay...was he? Gray himself had been with women when he was younger, trying to convince himself he didn't prefer men, but now he just couldn't imagine himself going to a female. That's why he couldn't figure out how a straight man could just all of a sudden decide --

"You're doing it again." Shane pressed up close behind him and took the KY and condom from his hand. One arm moved around Gray's chest and kisses trailed down Gray's neck to his shoulder.

Oh! That hard body aligned against his was heaven. He wiggled, rubbing that solid prick against his lower back. "Doing what?"

"Overanalyzing." Shane released him and leaned back.

Gray started to protest, but he heard foil tear and turned around in time to see Shane roll it on. Brown eyes caught his once the condom was in place. "This okay?" For the first time, Shane looked unsure of himself.

Well, that's interesting. But now was not the time for questions. Gray reached up and caressed one of those high cheekbones and smirked. "If you are asking if you can fuck me in the ass, then, yeah, it's okay."

Shane leaned forward and nipped Gray's bottom lip. "Don't be crude, Grayson." But he was smiling and pushed Gray forward, giving him no choice but to catch himself with his hands. Which apparently was what he'd intended, because he touched Gray's thigh, then popped the top on the lube. "Raise up."

"Bossy bastard," Gray mumbled.

Shane swatted him on the ass. "What was that?" The tube of KY landed on the bed beside Gray and Shane's slick fingers skimmed down his crease and over his anus.

"Nothing."

Gray gasped as one blunt finger pressed inside. Shane forged deeper, his long finger grazing Gray's prostate. *Goddamn!* Gray dropped to his elbows, resting his forehead on the bed between his forearms.

Shane groaned behind him, then his mane tickled the backs of Gray's legs as he bent and pressed his lips to the base of Gray's spine. "You've done this before, right?"

Shit! When was the last time he'd done this? Gray nodded, wiggling back, wanting more. He got it, too, as Shane started to move his finger in and out. He barely managed to get the words out. "Yeah. Have you?"

A second finger joined the first and another kiss landed on his back. "Shh…"

He was so damned turned on that that second finger hadn't even stung. He'd never felt more ready in his life. "Shane, please. Now!"

The fingers left and the silken heat of Shane's cock pressed against him, rubbing around his hole. Shane's other hand caressed his back. "Push out."

Gray did, knowing that it would make things easier, but how did --

Oh! The head of Shane's huge prick pushing in had stung a bit. Not badly, but he'd definitely felt that. Slowly, Shane glided all the way in, his thighs moving against Gray's. "Okay?"

Fuck yeah; it was more than okay. It felt so sublime he could barely get his mind together. His body had already adjusted to the invasion and, damn! Had he ever been this needy? That thick cock head brushed his gland again...this was not going to last long. Not at all.

"Grayson! Are you all right?" One hand massaged his back, the other stroked his hip.

How the hell could Shane sound so calm? "Yes, oh, God, yes! Would you fucking move already?"

Holy shit, did he move! The hand on Gray's hip grabbed hold, gripping tightly as he set up a steady rhythm, thrusting smoothly in and out. Shane's dick rubbed just right on every. Single. Damned. Stroke.

Oh, it was good! So freaking good! Gray's hands fisted the comforter and he bit his bottom lip. He was whimpering, but he couldn't care less. Shane's dick felt fucking wonderful! If only he could see his lover. The sound of Shane moaning and panting, the heat of Shane's body against his...it was too much. Gray was on sensory overload! His balls pulled impossibly tight and his spine actually began to tingle .

Shane's hand left his back and grasped Gray's cock, squeezing, pumping.

"Oh, fuck, Chief!" Gray rocked back and forth between the hand on his cock and the dick in his ass.

Shane's hand clamped onto Gray, his other hand moving faster in time with the snap of his hips. "That's it, Grayson. Come for me!"

He did. His hole clasped Shane rhythmically as he shot his load all over Shane's fingers and the comforter. And, fuck, if his eyes couldn't focus, he'd come so hard. He felt damned good, his body actually shaking. Quivering. Hell he was still spurting.

Shane suddenly stiffened behind him and let out a low, ragged groan. It was sexy as hell! Then he fell over Gray's back, his hair draping over his sides as he kissed Gray just below his shoulder blades. He pulled out bit by bit and lay down next to Gray before reaching over and pulled Gray into his body, spooning him. His top arm snaked around Gray's waist, hand pressing flat against Gray's stomach.

Gray lay there dazed and confused, but so relaxed he couldn't move his limbs if his life depended on it. What the hell had just happened? And how was it going to affect them from this point? He'd wanted the two of them to be friends again. Was Shane going to freak out on him once he got his breath back? Was he already regretting what they'd done? What if --

"Cut it out and go to sleep."

"Huh?"

"I can practically hear your brain spinning, Grayson. Go to sleep." His lips brushed Gray's shoulder.

Fuck it! He'd deal with the fall out when he woke up. "Night, Chief."

"Night, love."

Gray sighed. Too bad Shane hadn't really meant that.

* * *

Gray lay in the dark, blinking, trying to awaken fully. What in the holy hell had he done? He was no longer on top of the covers, but his back was still snuggled against Shane's front.

Boy, when he fucked up, he fucked up but good! No screwing up a little at a time for him, oh no! He just jumped right in, head first! Exactly the way he'd done when he was seventeen. What the hell was Chief gonna say about this? Never mind that Shane had actually started it. Somehow this was going to be Gray's fault; he just knew it. *Fuckin' A!* Stupid, stupid, stupid!

Gray scooted forward out of Shane's embrace, hoping like hell he still slept like the dead. Shane rolled onto his back, thankfully sound asleep. God, he was gorgeous, even with his hair all over the place. Those luscious lips were parted slightly, and his luscious black lashes lay against his cheeks.

Gray closed his eyes. He'd always loved Shane and had missed him incredibly. Yesterday, Shane had seemed pretty willing to accept him back into his life; had Gray destroyed that? He hoped not; he'd be willing, albeit reluctantly, to settle for a platonic relationship just to be near the man.

He gathered his clothes and dressed in the living room, then picked up his bag and left. Once he got to the big house, he left the lights off and went straight to his room, which appeared exactly the way he'd left it eleven years ago. He'd been in here a time or two over the years, but this was the first time he'd actually sleep here again since then.

Gray dropped his bag in a chair by the door, then stripped and crawled under the covers. He rolled over and glanced at the picture on his nightstand, able to make out the image in the moonlight filtering through his blinds. His dad, Shane, and he were all laughing. He had his arm around Shane's shoulder, and his dad was on Shane's other side. His mom had taken the picture at a Fourth of July celebration one year before Gray'd left.

He traced a finger down the glass over Shane's smiling face, then his dad's. It had been a great day, the four of them one big happy family. If he was lucky, all of them would pose for a similar picture this Fourth of July.

Chapter Four

The phone woke Shane. He rolled over and glanced at the clock as he grabbed the phone. *6:02 a.m.* "Hello?"

"Shane, honey, this is Aunt Tara."

He sat up, trying to wake fully. Why was Ted's sister calling him? "Hi, Aunt Tara." Shane glanced around the room, heated memories of last night coming back to him. Where was Grayson?

"Listen, honey, Kaitlyn called me last night to let me know about Ted and I was wondering if I could ride up to the hospital with you. I tried to call Gray but there was no answer. I can drive out to the Broken H and meet you; it's just I don't really want to drive all the way to San Antonio by myself."

"Sure, that would be fine. Grayson is here, too; he'll ride up to the hospital with us."

"Oh, good! All right, Shane, let me get ready and I'll see you in about forty minutes."

"Okay, Aunt Tara, see you then."

"Thanks, hon."

Shane hung up the phone and leaned back against the headboard. He'd always slept soundly, but to not feel Gray get out of bed...he must have been really out of it. But then, that wasn't surprising; yesterday had been one of the longest -- and yet best -- of his life.

Warily, he waited a few minutes for regret to creep in, but it never came. Being with Gray had felt...right. He hadn't planned it, but the younger man had stared at him with such intensity he hadn't been able to help himself. When Shane had taken a look into that handsome face and seen those bright green eyes focus hungrily on him, he'd known exactly what Gray felt. It had been written all over his face, the longing, the lust...the love. Suddenly, it had all become quite clear why Gray had left and why he'd stayed away. Almost as remarkably, Shane found that he himself was no longer afraid of his own feelings. In that moment before he'd called Grayson to come to him, everything had clicked.

Grayson still deserved someone better than Shane, but Shane admitted he was a selfish man. Making love to Grayson had been like nothing he'd ever experienced. Just being near the younger man made him feel good. In fact, Gray sort of always had been a salvation to him. More than once those bright green eyes had kept him going and showed him what life should be about: joy, love, enthusiasm, and more. The fact that he'd watched Gray grow up had constantly been an issue. Thirteen years had seemed an insurmountable gap back then, but now it just didn't seem that big a deal.

Shane wanted him. He'd always desired Gray in different ways, of course, but he'd always loved having the boy around. Gray had gone from being Shane's protégé to his friend...and now his lover.

He got out of bed and checked the house. Empty. He looked out the window and saw that Gray's truck was still there. Good. The man must have gone to the big house.

He had no idea why Gray had left his bed, but he wasn't going to let him put distance between them again. Not this time. He and Gray weren't through, but if Gray thought otherwise, he had another think coming. Unfortunately, he knew the stubborn cuss well enough to understand that he was going to have his work cut out for him. Shane looked forward to straightening his lover out.

Shane got ready, then checked the clock one last time. *6:27* He closed the door behind him and headed to the big house. It was still quiet on the ranch; the hands wouldn't be arriving for about another thirty minutes, just in time for him to give them their orders for the day and leave for the hospital.

He grinned. He had some time with Gray all to himself. Ted's surgery was set for 10:00 a.m. They all would have just enough time to get a bite to eat and get there before Ted was prepped for his operation. After Shane and Gray had spoken with the doctor the night before, they'd felt better about the surgery, but Shane knew he wasn't the only one who wasn't willing to not see Ted beforehand. The man had been in Shane's life far longer than his own father had.

A slight breeze blew some strands of his hair into his face. Crap. Somehow or another he'd lost that last damned rubber band. He thought Gray had put it on the kitchen counter, but naturally he couldn't find the blasted thing. Hell, maybe he'd go to the barber shop after Ted's surgery was over and he was sure the man was fine.

He entered the house and strode quickly to Ted's office, grabbed a handful of rubber bands out of Ted's top drawer, then stuffed all but one into the right front pocket of his jeans before climbing the main stairs to find Gray. As he took the stairs, he finger-combed his hair and separated it into three sections.

When he reached the landing, he heard the shower, and pictured Gray naked and wet. Oh, yeah, the morning was getting better by the moment. Shane's braid rapidly took shape as he pushed the bathroom door open with his hip just as the water cut off. He leaned against the door frame and waited.

It didn't take long, Gray pulled back the curtain and stepped out, reaching for his towel.

Damn, but he'd grown into a fine man. Hell, last night it had taken everything he had not to melt at the man's feet and he'd barely had the chance to really look him over. Now, though, the leisurely sight of that glistening body perked Shane's cock right up. Wide shoulders tapered down to lean hips and heavily muscled thighs. Gray's ass made Michelangelo's David's look plain uninspiring. Like Shane, Gray had very little body hair, just a bit on his arms and legs and a dark trail down the toned belly that led to his cock. There were a few scars here and there from his days on the rodeo circuit and the bullet scar on his right deltoid, but they were battle scars and served to enhance his beauty.

Gray ran the towel over his dark hair as his green eyes met Shane's in the mirror. "Chief."

"Grayson." He dipped his head. "Your Aunt Tara is going to ride to the hospital with us."

Gray nodded, then looked away.

Well, hell! He'd known Gray was going to be bristly, but he wasn't sure why exactly he'd be that way. Even if he was apprehensive about what he felt for Shane, there had to be something else bothering him for him to hightail it before Shane woke up. "You didn't have to leave."

"I thought you'd want me to." Gray bent to dry his legs, showing off that fine ass.

Shane barely held back a moan. The man seemed totally unaware of his appeal and the show he was giving Shane. In fact he looked...uncertain. "Why would I want that?"

Gray wrapped the towel around his waist and put his hands on his hips. "You're telling me you don't regret it?"

"I don't have any regrets about last night."

One dark eyebrow lifted. "None?"

"No. Why would I?" Shane raised a brow of his own.

Gray shook his head and grabbed the pile of clothes off the counter and started to dress. He was quiet for several minutes while he yanked on a white pullover shirt, red boxers and jeans. He brushed out his hair and brushed his teeth. The whole time there was a fine tension to him that most people would have missed. But Shane knew him, and it gave him an anxious feeling in his gut.

Gray finally turned and faced him, back against the counter, arms crossed over his chest, brow furrowed. "You don't like... I mean you've never..." He took a deep breath and let it out. "You aren't gay."

What? Shane was flabbergasted. "I'm not?" How could Gray not know? Shane pushed off the doorframe and stood in front of the younger man. He reached up and soothed the furrow with his thumb and met those worried green eyes. "I don't understand why you think that." He ran the backs of his fingers down one smooth cheek. Grayson leaned in to his touch, closing his eyes for a second before abruptly stepping away.

Shane let him retreat, sensing his need for space, his need to analyze. Gray had always been that way. On the surface, he'd appeared impulsive, but Shane knew better. Everything Gray did was well thought out. He smiled fondly. "There you go again, pondering things into the ground."

"You confuse me, Shane."

"You confuse me, too, so we're even."

"You're gay?"

"Have been for as long as I can remember."

"Why didn't you ever tell me? I always thought… You should have told me."

The man was going to cross every T and dot every I whether Shane wanted him to or not. He sighed. "Because by the time you were old enough to discuss that sort of thing, you'd already left."

Gray snatched a pair of white sneakers and socks off the closed lid of the toilet, then sat down and put them on. Shane didn't know what Gray was thinking but whatever it was, he knew his future hinged on it. "What do we do now?" Gray whispered.

"We take it one day at a time."

Gray leaned his elbows on his knees and stayed almost motionless for several minutes. Finally, he looked back at Shane. "I need you to be my friend, Shane. I can't lose that again."

Shane's stomach settled more easily; this was promising. He could deal with this, but he didn't fool himself into thinking it was going to be easy. Nothing with Gray ever was, but it was a good start. He wasn't going to push right now, not until they knew Ted was going to be okay and things got a little closer to being normal.

He smoothed his fingers through Gray's thick, dark-brown hair. There was just a hint of auburn in this light, but when the sun hit it, it looked almost as red as Kaitlyn's fiery hair. "I was always your friend, Grayson. It was you who pulled away from me. You're the one who left and didn't come back."

The sound of the back door shutting was followed by a female voice. "Boys? Where are you?"

Shane sighed. *Damn Aunt Tara's timing.*

Gray almost looked relieved at the interruption. He stood and slapped Shane on the shoulder. "Let's go to the hospital."

* * *

Gray laid his head back and closed his eyes, half listening to Aunt Tara chatter to his mom and Shane. The movement of the truck and the hum of the motor was almost soothing. Today had been another emotionally draining day. Although his dad's surgery had gone well and he was recovering, Gray'd be lying if he said he hadn't been worried. He had gotten to see his dad in the cardiac ICU after the operation, but Ted had still been asleep. Then, for a good thirty minutes, he'd argued with his mother about her staying at the hospital. Finally, the doctor had told her she couldn't stay in Ted's room, adding that Dad wouldn't be alert until the morning anyway. Only then had she agreed to go home and get a good night's sleep. Damn, the woman was stubborn!

Then there was him and Shane; things between them were still strained. They really hadn't settled anything before his aunt Tara had arrived at the ranch, and they hadn't had two minutes alone since then. He had no clue where he stood with Shane, and he'd almost felt betrayed that he hadn't known Shane was gay. All these years why had Shane led him to believe that he'd been disgusted by Gray coming on to him? Or had he? Had Gray misunderstood? If he were honest with himself, he didn't remember much about the actual details, just the feelings of rejection and loss.

"Shane, honey, what is that there in the --" The truck swerved. Both the women gasped while Shane spat out an expletive.

Gray's eyes flew open; instinctively, he grabbed the steering wheel to get them back on the road.

Shane slapped his hand. "I got it!"

Gray frowned and moved back into his seat after seeing Shane really did have everything under control. "What the hell was that?"

"Nothing." Shane grumbled. "Sorry, everyone."

Kaitlyn leaned forward. "Shane, are you tired? Why don't you pull over and let Gray drive the rest of the way home."

Shane's jaw tightened. "I'm okay, Kaitlyn. I just didn't see it."

See what? Gray glanced out the back window and saw the dead cow lying in the road about thirty yards back. "Hell, Shane, I can see if from here. Are you dozing off?"

Shane's shoulders were stiff and...was he squinting? "No, I'm not dozing off. I'm wide awake." He *was* squinting.

Gray checked the path ahead of them and realized they were only about half a mile from home. "You need to get your eyes seen to."

A muscle in Shane's jaw ticked.

Shit. That hadn't come out right. "What I mean is, you might need glasses now that you're older. A lot of people --"

Shane turned his head and glared at him, eyebrow cocked, eyes narrowed. "Do you want to drive?" His tone made it quite clear that the answer better be no, then he returned his attention to the road.

Gray sighed and shook his head. "No." They were almost home. There was no sense in starting an argument over it now.

His mother, God bless her, defused the tension. She patted Shane on the shoulder and chuckled. "Well, I didn't see it either until we were right up on it. Good thing I wasn't driving, I'd have probably hit it. That wasn't one of our cows, was it, Shane?"

"No, ma'am, that was a Jersey; we only have Herefords and Red Angus."

Gray barely suppressed a snort. Honestly, she could have been less obvious. His mother knew darned well what kind of cattle the Broken H raised and the woman had eyes like a hawk. There was no way she could confuse those breeds, but he was thankful for her distraction anyhow. For some reason, his eyesight was a sore point with Shane, but someone was going to have to bring it up again. Shane really did need to get his eyes inspected. That cow had been pretty visible, smack dab in the middle of the road as it was. Well, it should have been. Obviously, Shane wasn't the only one having a hard time seeing it; someone had hit it, after all.

They pulled into the drive and Shane parked the truck. He got out and opened the door for Aunt Tara and Gray did likewise for his mother. The women soon headed into the house, leaving them alone on the gravel. Gray leaned against the truck, his arms folded across his chest. "So, you want to tell me what that was all about?"

Shane's eyes flashed fire at him. "No. I want to take my decrepit ass home and go to bed." He turned and strode off angrily, leaving Gray to stare after him.

What the fuck?!

Chapter Five

Shane made it all the way to the front door and had stuck his key in the lock before his brain decided to override his pride. His eyesight *was* getting bad, but he'd actually been lost in thought and not paying attention to his driving or he *would* have seen that damned cow sooner. Still, damned if that age comment hadn't riled him up but good.

All right. He took a deep breath and let it out slowly. He was exhausted and on edge from watching the people he loved suffer all day. Ted had looked so old and helpless, not at all like the robust man Shane knew. In the surgical recovery room, he'd been unconscious and on a respirator while Kaitlyn had stayed at his side, holding his hand with tears in her eyes, and described the room and its occupants to the unresponsive man. She'd been strong for all their sakes, but her worry was clear.

Getting older positively sucked. Seeing Ted and Kaitlyn and Tara had reminded Shane of his own mortality. He could easily picture him and Gray in the same situation, as their age difference was nearly the same as Kaitlyn and Ted's. He never wanted Gray to go through what his mother had endured today. Shane had determined that he would put everything behind him and vowed to take better care of himself than Ted had. And then Gray had reminded him that he was aging.

Shane banged his forehead on the door. Twice. *Damn it!* "Grayson!" He knew Gray hadn't moved, but he turned from the door to see him.

Sure enough, the other man was still standing where Shane had left him, staring back at Shane and looking confused as hell. "Yeah?"

"Come inside…please."

Gray nodded and strode toward him.

Shane let out the breath he hadn't realized he was holding, pivoted to the door and swung it wide. He desperately needed a beer. He crossed the living room, flipped on the lamp by the couch and continued into the kitchen. Grabbing two bottles from the fridge, he tossed the bottle cap from his onto the counter and took a long pull. Resting against the counter, he took another swig, draining half the bottle, then heard the front door click shut.

Gray appeared in the kitchen seconds later. Shane held out the unopened bottle and took another drink from his own. Gray opened his drink and flipped the cap next to Shane's on the counter. He swung one of the kitchen chairs backward and straddled it before gulping another drink, then dangling the bottle in his fingers. Resting his arms on the back of the chair, he glanced at Shane.

Shane heaved a sigh, set down his beer and hoisted himself up to sit facing Gray. He sipped some more beer while gathering his thoughts. It was time to discuss what was between the two of them. Hell, all day they hadn't had a chance to snatch even a few precious seconds to talk, and that was probably one reason why he was so damn short tempered.

"I'm sorry, I shouldn't have snapped at you. I had my mind on other things and was only half paying attention to the road. But you're right, I do need to get my eyes examined." He pinched the bridge of his nose.

Gray raised a brow and took another drink.

"I..." He what? Didn't want to be too old for Gray? That's what it boiled down to, after all. He was getting ahead of himself. "We need to talk about last night."

"Yeah. I guess we do, but I don't really want to."

"It's not going away if you ignore it."

Gray snorted. "No shit, Chief. I've been trying to ignore how I feel for close to twelve years, and it sure as hell hasn't gone away."

Twelve years? What was Gray talking about? "Well, then, I reckon it's time you faced it. Talk."

Gray rested his chin on the chair back, twirled the beer bottle, swished the liquid. He was quiet for several moments, then he looked up at Shane, eyebrows drawn together. "Why?"

"Why what?"

"Why everything? Why last night? Why what happened eleven some years ago? Why did you let me leave?" Gray's voice seemed to tremble a little on the last question. He chugged his beer, clearly trying to pretend it hadn't.

Whoa! "All right, I'm lost; you said that like you expected me to keep you here. I don't understand, Grayson. How was I supposed to do that?"

Gray sighed. "You didn't want me and pushed me away all those years ago. So why have you all of a sudden decided that you do want me? What's changed?"

"I've always wanted you. At first it was just because I loved you. Then, as you grew older, it turned to lust, too. There has never been a day that's gone by that I don't want you around."

Gray stood, tossed back the rest of his beer, then set it on the table with a thud before taking another out of the fridge. Once he was seated again, he looked at Shane, his gaze hard. "The summer I turned seventeen, we went fishing together. You remember?"

Shane shook his head. "We always went fishing together."

"No, this time was different. We'd been talking. I was telling you about my break up with, oh, hell, what was her name, the little blond. Christy? Yeah, that was it, Christy. I kept trying to tell you why I went from girlfriend to girlfriend, but you wouldn't listen. You kept interrupting me. So, I tried to kiss you and you --"

Oh, fuck! Shane dropped his head in his hands. Now he remembered it perfectly. Gray had kept trying to tell him he was gay and Shane had kept trying not to hear. He thought he'd somehow influenced Gray. It had bothered him terribly that Gray had tried to kiss him...because he'd wanted it so damned bad. He'd even thought he must have manipulated Gray into it, not to mention that Gray had been too damned young to know what the hell he wanted at the time.

Afterward, Shane had half convinced himself that it had never happened, that it had all been his wishful thinking.

Shane dropped his hands and looked up. "And I ignored that, too. That's why you left?"

"Yeah."

"I'm sorry. I never meant to hurt you. I...you were so young, Grayson."

Gray's mouth gaped just a bit, then his jaw clenched and he glared at Shane. "That's it, isn't it? That's what that little episode in the truck was about, too. You think you're too old for me. Well, fuck you, Shane!" Gray rose and stomped out the back door, slamming it behind him.

Shane wanted to follow, but forced himself to stay put. They best way to deal with Gray had always been to let him work things out himself. Either he would get over being pissed, or he'd get madder. One way or another, he'd eventually come back. At least, he'd always done so before... Well, that was then, but he didn't think Gray would have changed all that much. Shane sighed. What the hell was he supposed to do now?

He finished his beer, opened another, then parked his old, tired ass on the couch.

Son of a bitch! He'd spent all those years away for nothing. Wasted time when he could have spent them with Shane. Damn, Shane anyway! Gray took a swig of beer, then stared at the bottle. He seriously considered hurling it across the yard, but then he'd have to go pick it up, not to mention probably have to fend off his mom and aunt's questions. He blew out a breath and turned the bottle upside down, letting the drink flow out onto the ground. Suddenly, he just didn't feel like drinking. He was afraid if he continued, he wouldn't stop, and drinking never solved anything, especially when you were doing it to drown your sorrows or regrets or whatever the fuck else.

He stepped off the porch and headed toward the barrels by the barn. There wasn't any trash service out here so you burned your garbage or recycled. Glasses in one barrel, aluminum in another, paper and perishables in the "burn barrel" and plastics in yet another. *What a pain in the ass!* He'd never minded going out to burn trash as a kid, that had been fun, but he sure as hell hated having to sort the shit. He found the glass barrel and chucked the bottle in, satisfied with the sharp clink and crash when it broke.

He wandered over to the fence, listening to the sounds of the night, taking everything in. Even with the sun down it was hot, but there was nice breeze, so it was bearable. In some ways, he'd really missed the ranch. He'd missed the peacefulness, the stars, the sound of crickets and critters at night. The skeeters were probably going to suck him dry, but he didn't care. He needed to get away; he needed to think.

He carefully climbed through the barbed wire along the fencing and kept going. With the moon lighting his way, he could see just fine. It really was pretty land. He had no real direction in mind, or so he tried to tell himself. He hated to admit it, but even while riding the rodeo circuit and spending time in San Antonio, he'd been homesick for all of this. Shane and his parents hadn't been the only things he'd missed.

Damn it! Why had Shane let him go over something so stupid? How could the man have possibly thought that he was too old, or that age even mattered? Hell, Shane hadn't even known why Gray had taken off. All this time, he'd carried around the hurt and rejection and Shane hadn't even had a fucking clue. What did that mean? Apparently, he wasn't even worth Shane getting upset over.

Gray sighed when the stock pond came into view. He hadn't been here since that day, and obviously the entire event was only a bad memory for *him*. "Fuck!"

Something stirred in the grass and moved away. He probably should have brought a gun, but no way in hell was he going back for it now. Snakes and coyotes be damned. The mood he was in he'd just jump on them and rip them to shreds with his bare hands if any decided to bother him.

Gray sank down to the ground and pulled his knees up to his chest as he surveyed the moonlit water. It was so serene here that it was hard to believe this was the spot where he'd made a decision that had disrupted a large part of his life. Not that it had been all bad. He'd never have gone and ridden bulls if it hadn't happened, and he damned sure wouldn't have been a lawman.

He couldn't regret those things; they'd helped to make him who he was. He'd really discovered who he was while riding the circuit and he'd made some friends. He'd also, as the saying went, sowed some wild oats. And, of course, he'd won enough money to put himself through college and get a bachelor's degree in criminal justice. His parents would have gladly paid for his schooling, but he'd wanted to make his own way. He'd tested with the force in San Antonio, then they'd put him through the academy. He'd spent four years there, then he'd returned home, ran for sheriff and, wham, the rest was history. He still wasn't sure why he'd come back instead of staying in San Antonio. No, that wasn't true; he'd come back to be near Shane. Not that he'd ever have admitted it at the time, but in the back of his mind he'd always held out hope that someday, Shane would forgive him and maybe even love him.

Gray snorted and lay back in the grass, staring up at the stars and listening to the breeze move the water. That was his problem, of course; despite his years as a cowboy and, later, an officer, he was a still fucking hopeless romantic. How pathetic was that? Even that frickin' day, sitting just a few yards away from where he was now, he'd somehow convinced himself that Shane felt the same way he had.

He'd just caught a fish and started reeling it in when Shane's hand landed on his shoulder, then his other tried to snag the fishing pole.

"Quick! You're going to lose it! Reel it in, Grayson!"

"I am!" He laughed and kept reeling, then jerked the pole back, but still lost the fish. But he and Shane got a good chuckle out of it on account that Gray stepped back, lost his footing and slid in the mud.

Shane cackled so hard the man nearly lost his own fishing pole when he got a bite on the forgotten line lying on the bank. He and Shane both fell all over the place trying to get the pole before it disappeared into the water. In the end, Shane lost his fish, too.

They scooted back up the bank and lay in the grass, side by side, still chuckling. After they fell quiet, he tried to tell Shane he was gay, but Shane kept changing the subject. Gray was frustrated to no end and pretty certain that Shane knew damned well what Gray wanted to tell him, but he let it go.

He and Chief spent most of the rest of the afternoon not saying a word, just fishing.

Funny how Shane had always been one of the few people Gray could just relax with and not feel uncomfortable or awkward. With Chief, it was more like a companionable silence, like they knew what the other was thinking so really didn't need to say anything.

Shane eventually sat up and got them both a Coke from the cooler they'd brought down with them. Somehow or another when their hands had touched as Shane handed the beverage over, Gray had decided to kiss Shane.

Why had he done that? Gray jerked upright, blindly staring out over the water. He thought hard for a minute, trying to remember things about that day he'd always tried to forget. Why had he felt like it was a good idea to kiss Shane? He closed his eyes, sifting his memories. He could almost picture Shane's face just as it was that day. Shane had leaned into him first! Indeed, Chief had licked his lips and tilted his head just a fraction. Gray's hands had touched Shane's chest, caressing just briefly, before Shane had covered his hands with his. For just a second, Gray had thought Shane was holding them there to savor the sensation, then he'd shoved Gray away, a look of absolute horror on his face.

Gray's eyes flew open. How had he forgotten that? He'd completely overlooked the fact that Shane had more or less made the first move. Instead, he'd obsessed about what he had thought was Shane's rejection.

Shane mumbled an apology as he reared back. But Gray didn't stick around; he felt like such an idiot. He couldn't get the look of horror on Shane's face out of his head. He sprinted back to the big house and locked himself in his room where he made the decision to leave as soon as he graduated and turned eighteen.

At dinner -- Shane always ate dinner with the Hunters -- Shane asked him if he wanted to go fishing again the next day. Gray got pissed off all over again that Shane had already put the incident behind him. Chief was acting just as he always had, like Gray's friend, his protector.

"Shit!" What if Shane's horrified expression was due to disgust with himself rather than anger with Gray? Gray flung himself back in the grass again, gazing at the stars but not really seeing them. That was it! It had to be. Now things were beginning to make more sense. He ran his hands down his face, relaxing just a little as he remembered a scene from his childhood.

He was seven, sitting on Shane's shoulder as they walked up and down the stable aisles at a livestock auction. Chief was nineteen or twenty and had both his hands securely around Gray's ankles while Gray's hands were wrapped around Shane's forehead.

In one of the stalls, there was a beautiful brown Tobiano Paint. Gray fell head over heels in love. He had to have that horse. He tapped Shane's head and pointed. "There, Chief! That one! I want that one. I'm going to name him Thunder! That's the perfect horse for a brave."

Shane chuckled and went to the stall to have a better look. They got too close and the horse shied away. Shane stepped back, too. "I don't know, Grayson. I don't think this horse is broke. Why don't we look around a little more?"

"No."

"Aw, come on, Grayson. Besides that, this is a mare. You can't name a girl horse Thunder. Thunder is a name more fitting to a stallion or a gelding."

Gray shook his head so hard that Shane squeezed his hands around the boy's ankles and moved to compensate for the movements.

Shane sighed again and called out to Ted.

Dad joined them in no time. "What's up, Shane?"

Shane pointed at the mare.

Gray did, too. "That one, Daddy."

Ted looked resigned. "I already asked about that one, Gray. She's a two-year-old that's barely green broke."

Gray tapped Shane on the head again and leaned down, forcing Shane to grab Gray's back, lest he fall off Shane's shoulders. "That one. It has to be that one, Chief."

Shane turned to Ted. "I'll finish breaking the horse if you tell me how. I know I can do it."

Ted frowned up at his son, then glanced back at Shane. "I don't know, Shane."

"I just need someone to guide me, Ted. You know if I say I'll do it, I will."

Ted looked once more at Gray and sighed. "Katy will have my head if you get hurt, Shane." He shook his head and walked off, mumbling under his breath. "You spoil that boy."

And that had been that. Gray had gotten his first horse, and Shane had gotten to break his first horse.

He rose from the ground and dusted himself off. Why hadn't he seen it before? Dad had been right; Shane had always acted as his protector and had spoiled him, too. Looking at their relationship from that perspective, Gray had no trouble seeing why anything resembling intimacy might have been difficult for Shane. It wasn't just the age difference, of course. Gray had always been Shane's responsibility, albeit self-imposed, but still... Shane had wanted him, probably had for a while. Gray no longer had any doubts about that. He knew Shane well enough to know that that day by the pond had likely made Shane believe he was taking advantage of the teenager Gray had been.

Somehow the thought that Shane had looked after him, had cared for him enough to protect Gray even from Shane himself, made Gray feel much better about the situation. Ironically, what Shane had never understood was that the only person Gray had never wanted or needed protecting from was Shane.

Gray trotted back to Shane's cottage, making a trip by the stables to see Thunder, then by the big house to retrieve his clothes for the following day. He wasn't letting what he thought Shane felt run him off this time, and he wasn't going to let his own insecurities do it, either. Shane was his, always had been, and Gray was going to make sure Shane realized it as well.

Chapter Six

Something disturbed him.

Shane blinked his bleary eyes open to find Gray removing Shane's boots as he reclined on the couch. After Gray tugged the second boot off his foot, Shane sat up and yawned.

"Didn't mean to wake you, Chief." Gray seated himself on the end of the couch.

"'S okay." Shane glanced at the clock. *2 a.m.* About a couple of hours after Gray stormed out. "You want to talk yet?" Shane stretched his hands over his head and twisted side to side, making his vertebrae pop.

Gray nodded. "I thought you were disgusted when you pushed me away. I thought you didn't want anything to do with me after I tried to kiss you. I was embarrassed and I guess I let that color my perception."

Shane grinned. That was his boy! Always so responsible. He'd never been one to not admit when he was wrong, but Shane wasn't letting him take this one by himself. If there was blame to go around, then Shane had accept some, too. Probably more than Gray, if truth be told. "It's my fault, too, Grayson. I could have done a lot of things differently. I should have sat you down and demanded to know what was wrong. I had plenty of opportunity to do so before you left, but I just didn't trust myself to keep my hands off you. I didn't want you to do anything you might regret, but I admit I also thought you were going through a phase or that I'd somehow projected my feelings and desires onto you."

Gray shut his eyes briefly, a serene little smile on his face, and nodded. After several silent moments, he said, "You aren't old."

Shane wanted to crawl across the couch and kiss that grin from his mouth; instead, he found himself smiling back. That was all he'd needed, to hear Gray acknowledge he understood why Shane had done and said the things he'd did made him feel better about it. "Truce?"

Those green eyes blinked open, practically dancing. "Truce. Where do we go from here?"

"Where do you want to go from here?"

The grin Gray gave him should have clued him in, but Shane was just so thrilled to have that particular look turned on him for the first time in years that he didn't see it coming.

"Bed."

"Excuse me?" No way could it be this simple. Gray never did anything the easy way. Sure the younger man had always weighed the consequences before he acted, but he still did things *his* way. Which was not necessarily how others wanted them done, including Shane.

"Bed."

"Bed? As in sex or as in sleeping?"

"Both, actually." Gray got up and held his hand out to Shane.

Shane took it, letting Gray pull him up. He was as confused. He'd been positive Gray would want to take things slow, and he'd resigned himself to it. But damn if the man hadn't just thrown him for a loop.

They stood there for several seconds, staring into each other's eyes, then Gray leaned forward and kissed him. It wasn't a deep kiss or overly lingering, but Shane was positive he'd never had its equal. Somehow the mood had shifted and everything felt...right. "Okay, let's go." He was surprised, not stupid; there was no way he was going to turn that offer down.

The smile Gray gave him was blinding. "I feel sticky from being outside. I'll lock the back door while you go start the shower. I already went and got my stuff and left Mom and Aunt Tara a note saying we'd meet them at the hospital tomorrow around nine."

"You're gonna sleep here?"

Gray winked. "I plan on it."

Damn, that look was enough to give a man a raging case of hormones. Shane silently told his libido to shut the hell up and beamed back at Gray.

"Be right back...old man." Gray hightailed into the kitchen, trailing chuckles behind him.

Shane groaned and grabbed his boots. *The little shit!* He should have known better than to confess his insecurity to Gray. Now he was going to have to endure endless old men remarks and jokes.

He dropped his footwear by his closet, continued on to the bathroom and started the shower. It wasn't long before he heard Gray fumbling around in the bedroom.

Shane laid out a couple of towels, stripped and got under the water. He tilted his face up into the spray and was reaching for the shampoo bottle when a small draft stopped him, followed by the *snick* of the shower door. Two arms soon wrapped around him from behind. Shane pulled his face out of the water and leaned back against Gray's strong body, which fit against Shane like he was born to it.

Gray's hard prick pressed against his butt and his chin came to rest on Shane's shoulder. Shane reached over his head and wound his arms around Gray's neck. His own dick stiffened at Gray's nearness. The very knowledge that he had the object of his lust with him and all the time in the world to explore was a heady feeling. He dropped his head back and pulled Gray forward, then turned his head to kiss him. Gray opened right up, moaning when their tongues touched.

Gray ran his hands up and down Shane's chest. Shane closed his eyes and relaxed. His lover's hands felt so good; he had strong hands, big and calloused, like Shane's own. They caressed over Shane's chest and stomach, never quite straying where Shane wanted them to.

Just as Gray's fingers skimmed over the tip of Shane's fully erect cock, he stopped rubbing and reached over Shane's shoulder, grabbing something off the shelf in front of them. A cap clicked open and the scent of vanilla surrounded them. *Shampoo.*

Gray kissed his shoulder and began to soap his hair. He massaged Shane's scalp, fingers lingering. "Love your hair,

Chief." Gray's lips met his shoulder again, then he continued to lather up Shane's hair.

Shane couldn't help the moan that escaped. Gray had great hands, gentle and firm at the same time. Even with an erection, it was relaxing. He could almost go to sleep right here.

"Close your eyes and tilt your head back." Gray pulled the shower nozzle off the wall and rinsed Shane's hair, then replaced it before picking up the mesh sponge and shower gel. "Turn around." Gray tugged on his arm.

Shane stood there, eyes closed, and simply enjoyed feeling Gray's hands on his body. The sponge traced his shoulders, pecs and stomach. Gray's palm followed, exploring, learning.

"Got a great body, Shane. You always have. I've been wanting to do this for a long time. Just run my hands all over you, touch you."

Oh, damn, what a confession. Shane moaned, leaning deeper into the caresses. Gray made him feel like a god. Soapy hands slid down his belly, stopping to circle his belly button, then toyed with the dark curls above his cock. "Oh..."

The adoration in that voice had Shane's eyes opening. Gray was staring, apparently mesmerized, his hands roaming restlessly over Shane's torso. He trailed one finger up Shane's harder-than-nails prick, then back down before he enclosed his fist over it.

Shane's stomach clenched, and his breath hitched.

Gray's eyes flew to his: beautiful eyes full of awe. He held Shane in his hand -- not stroking, not squeezing -- just held him. His other hand rested over Shane's heart. Surely Gray must be able to feel how hard Shane's heart was pounding.

Shane reached up, trailing his fingers down Gray's face. Sometimes it was hard to see the little boy he'd so adored in this adult face in front of him. He could almost forget who Gray was if it weren't for the eyes. Those green, green eyes. Shane skimmed a finger over the his lover's eyelids, along straight perfect nose, down to the shallow, barely there cleft in Gray's chin. He traced his finger over Gray's bottom lip.

Gray gasped, bringing Shane's gaze back to his. He leaned into Shane's hand, giving Shane no choice but to cup his cheek. When he spoke, his voice a whisper, almost a question, and it was full of wonder. "You think you aren't good enough for me."

Shane stilled. "No one is good enough for you, Grayson." He brushed a kiss across Gray's lips. "No one ever has been."

Gray moaned and pushed into his arms, pressing his strong hard body against Shane's, then devoured Shane's mouth, pushing needy little sounds into it. The hand still on Shane's prick stroked. Gray pulled back, biting Shane's flesh between the neck and shoulder. Just like that, they'd gone from a slow, exploratory loving to this heated passion.

Shane shivered. "Jesus! Let's get out of the shower before we fall down."

Gray continued raining kisses and bites over his shoulders and chest. "Yeah, Chief. Yeah. Want you."

"Anything you wish, love." Shane extracted himself from Gray long enough to hose off the remaining soap from both of them and shut down the water.

Gray opened the shower door and grabbed the towels, swiftly drying himself, then helping Shane dry his hair and body. Shane grinned and let him, watching Gray's pretty cock bob with every move he made and the flex of those big thigh muscles as Gray bent. "Enough. Come on. We will likely need another shower after we get wet again."

Gray chuckled, put his shoulder into Shane's abdomen in a fireman's lift and stood, carrying Shane into the bedroom. Shane sputtered, trying to decide whether to laugh or protest. But before he could do either, Gray dropped him onto the bed and immediately plastered himself on top of Shane, kissing the breath out of him.

Eventually, Gray sat up, straddling Shane's hips and leaning over him toward the nightstand. He removed the lube and condoms, piling everything on the bed before contemplating Shane. "Do we need the condoms? I have test results, less than a month old, at home, and I haven't been with anyone in well over six months or so."

Shane closed his eyes, taking a deep breath. Did this mean... "Grayson, if we do this, it's just us...ever. You understand? Are you okay with that?"

Gray smiled. "Are you trying to tell me we're an us? A couple?"

"I'm not telling you anything. I'm asking. 'Speak now or forever hold your peace' kind of asking."

Gray's lip quirked. "I do!" He picked up the condoms and flung them off the bed. They hit the wooden floor with soft sounds. He smiled widely at Shane. "Guess this means you're clean?"

Shane nodded, unable to keep from grinning, too. "There should be a record in my office filing cabinet under 'medical.'"

Gray kissed him, long and hard. When he came up for air, he raised his eyebrows. "You aren't expecting me to actually get up and look, are you?" He frowned and his lips tightened.

Shane chuckled. He'd seen that look, the "I don't wanna" look, off and on over the years ever since Gray was four. Just to be contrary, he really should make Gray go check, but that would be like cutting off his nose to spite his face. He reached up and wrapped his hand around the back of Gray's neck, pulling him back down. As he did so, Gray's hot, hard prick left a wet trail on his stomach. Oh, damn. He bucked his own hips, mashing his dick against Gray's firm belly.

Gray gasped and nipped his jaw before moving upright again. Snatching the lube, he squirted some onto his hand, then tossed it aside. He gripped Shane's prick, slicking him up, making his cock jerk at the contact.

Gray let go, then used his fingers to reach behind him to slick himself up.

Shane's eyes widened, staring into the beloved face above him. He hadn't expected that. He'd thought Gray was going to take him this time. Not that he was complaining; he'd always preferred to "top" his partners, but he would never deny his lover anything. "Grayson?"

"Yeah?" Gray scooted forward, positioning himself above Shane's cock, then slowly sank down.

Shane groaned and willed himself to be still while that tight heat gripped him, took him in. "Oh, God!"

Gray bit his bottom lip, eyes closed, a blissful look on his face. Finally, after a long moment, his lids lifted. Gray's ass rested on Shane's hips. "Did you say something?"

Did he? He couldn't remember. He shook his head and grabbed Gray's hips, urging him to continue, to move. Whatever it was could wait until his brain was working again because right now all he could think about was the tight grasp of Gray's hole squeezing him. He lifted his rear up and pulled Gray down.

Gray groaned and lay down over him, kissing his jaw, then he rolled them over so that Shane was on top. Shane didn't waste any time; he got his knees under him while Gray raised his own. Gray's thick, red prick was there between them, hard as you please, begging to be stroked. Shane clasped the throbbing shaft, pumping steadily, watching his lover's face.

Gray was sprawled out beneath him, looking like a debauched angel, those lust filled green eyes glazed over. He pushed himself toward Shane, almost whimpering, and constricted his muscles around Shane's dick. "Please, Chief. Move. Fuck me."

He did. He couldn't have stopped himself after a plea like that. Shane used one hand to brace himself above Gray and the other to slide along Gray's cock.

Gray moaned and squirmed, begging him and moving. "Oh, God, Yeah! Harder!"

Shane was happy to comply. He propelled himself into Gray harder and harder, reveling in the sensation of that firm ass squeezing him. His balls slapped against Gray at first, but then drew tighter. Every movement seemed new somehow. Not physically, of course, he'd done this countless times but, knowing that his partner was Gray, *his Grayson*, made this indescribably better.

"Now. Oh! Now, Shane. Now, now, now!" Gray's back bowed off the bed, his mouth opened on a gasp. The throbbing in Gray's hot flesh increased and it got more and more intense until finally he came, just like that. Semen splashed over Gray's chiseled abs, mixing in the trail of dark hair leading to his groin even as he took Shane with him into bliss. Shane's hips slammed forward one last time; he came -- for the first time ever without a condom -- into his lover's ass, then collapsed on top of Gray, knowing Gray could handle his weight. His lover's arms surrounded, hugging him like he'd never let go. Which was more than fine with Shane.

Shane kissed Gray's shoulder, rubbing his face against the other man's chest, then rolled over, slipping wetly from Gray's body as he did so. Scooting up, he snuggled the younger man's head against his own chest. He loved the way Gray felt in his arms. Hell, maybe he *was* old. But as long as Gray didn't mind the thirteen years between them, he wasn't going to let it bother him.

"'Night, old man."

Shane smiled against the dark-brown hair, kissed the top of Gray's head and pinched Gray's arm. "'Night, you little shit!"

Chapter Seven

"I look like an idiot!"

Gray grinned and leaned over Shane's shoulder, peering into the little mirror on the optometrist's assistant's desk. "I don't think so, Chief. I think they make you look...distinguished, sexy even."

Shane snorted. "Distinguished is just a fancy word for old."

Gray chuckled and stood up. "I give!"

The assistant, her name tag said, "Rosy," winked at Gray. "I agree with him, Mr. Cortez. I think they are very attractive on you."

Shane rolled his eyes at them both while he still examined his reflection. "Well, I don't guess it matters, anyway. I can see and that's what counts."

"That's right. So, get used to them because I'm going to tell my deputies to stop you and harass you every time they see you driving without them." And he would, too. He'd be damned if he let Shane's vanity get him killed.

Shane glared at him in the mirror. "You wouldn't dare!"

Gray shrugged and quirked a brow. He didn't want to get into this now. They needed to get a bite, then return to the hospital. But since they were already at the mall, maybe they'd look around and find his dad some sort of get well gift. He nudged Shane's shoulder. "Come on, old man, we have places to go, stomachs to fill and people to see."

Shane frowned at his mirror reflection one last time, then stood, grumbling something under his breath that sounded suspiciously like, "little shit." He thanked Rosy, took the glasses case she offered him and turned and pushed Gray toward the door.

Once they got out of the LensCrafters store and into the mall, Gray leaned over and whispered in Shane's ear. "You really *do* look hot in those glasses, Chief. They make you look really smart."

Shane thumped Gray on his shoulder. "I *am* really smart."

Gray smiled. That much was true. From what Gray knew, Shane had taken all advanced placement classes in high school and graduated at the top of his class a year early. He'd turned down a full academic scholarship to the University of Texas so he could replace the Broken H's elderly foreman. Shane had had a head for business and the ranch had flourished under his management. Gray had never met anyone that could do math in their head faster than Shane, and as a teenager, Gray had taken full advantage of it. His philosophy had been who needed a calculator when he had Shane. Unfortunately, it hadn't taken Shane long to figure out why Gray followed him around with his algebra homework in hand. Yeah, Chief had put a stop to that pretty quick.

Gray leaned in close again so that only Shane could hear him. "Yup, I know, but did you know I have a thing for sexy smart guys? Do you have any idea what I'd like to do to those glasses?"

A smile tugged at Shane's lips, and he raised an eyebrow. "With them on my face or off?"

"Well, what fun would it be to do it with them off?"

Shane's steps faltered, and he cleared his throat. "Behave. Good Lord, I had no idea you were such a pervert and you an officer of the law, too." He tsked.

Gray would have kept teasing but his pants were getting a little tight in the zipper area, and he really didn't want to be walking through the mall with a boner.

"Besides, I'd rather you show me than tell me." Shane winked, his hand brushing against Gray's briefly.

Gray growled. Yeah, he actually freaking growled. Damn Shane, Gray's cock was not going to get any softer with that little remark.

"Problems, Grayson?"

"Just one." He smiled, baring his teeth and fluttering his lashes.

Shane shook his head, grinning from ear to ear. "But you'd have to clean them afterward."

Huh? "Clean what?"

"My glasses."

Gray groaned. "Oh, God…"

A clopping noise came up fast behind them, then a hand landed on his shoulder and Shane's from behind. It startled the arousal right out of him. He pivoted sharply to find Jamie Killian.

"Keep walking! Go, go, go…" Jamie wore a pair of khaki shorts that hung just above his knees, a white Kenny Chesney T-shirt, a beige ball cap and a pair of flip flops, hence explaining the clopping noise. He looked at the direction he came from them, then gave both Shane and Gray a little nudge to get them moving again.

Shane chuckled and obliged him by walking forward. "Hey, Jamie. What are you doing here?"

"Birthday present shopping. How 'bout y'all?" Jamie's forehead creased as he squeezed between them. "You know, I don't think I've ever seen the two of you together." He shrugged and peered at Gray. "How's your daddy?"

Gray glanced behind them to see if he could figure out who Jamie was hiding from. "He had a double bypass yesterday, but he's doing good. We went to see him this morning in CCU. He was still pretty out of it after they took him off the ventilator, so we came to do some shopping and get some grub, then we're going back."

"Great, glad to hear it. I like your dad. He's a nice guy. You need anything? I ordered some flowers to be sent up to the hospital this morning."

"Thank you, Jamie."

"You're welcome. I didn't figure your dad would care too much for the flowers, but I know your mama will like them. And at least he'll know we're thinking about him." Jamie cast a furtive glance over his shoulder.

Shane looked as well, then shook his head, grinning. "Who are you buying a birthday present for? And who are you hiding from?"

"Ethan. Oh, hey, that reminds me, Gray. You still coming over to play poker next Tuesday night?"

Gray shrugged and eyed Shane. Jamie did, too. Then his eyes went from Gray to Shane again, obviously putting two and two together and coming up with the correct result. A huge smile appeared on his face and he chuckled.

"Shane, of course, is welcome to join us. I was planning on having cake and ice cream since Ethan's birthday is the next day, but don't bring presents. He made me promise I wouldn't throw a birthday party. Just get some beer or snacks or something."

Shane smiled. "We'd love to come."

"Cool!" Jamie clapped Shane on the back. "You'll have to start coming to our weekly poker games. Right now it's just me, Ethan, Gray, John and Royal. Sometimes Bill and sometimes one of our three hands, but there's always room for one more."

Gray chuckled at Jamie's excitement. "Come on, spill. Who the heck are you hiding from?"

"Julia. She made me go into Victoria's Secret." Jamie gave an exaggerated shudder. "God, I don't know what was the worst, the lady with the huge boobs and way too much perfume flirting with me, the creepy bald biker guy leering at me while he was waiting for his girlfriend or the three girl teens asking me if I preferred thong panties or bikini bottoms." He shuddered again and made loud gagging noises.

Gray and Shane cracked up.

"Yeah, you two laugh, but y'all didn't have to experience it! I mean, it was bad enough that she made me go in there in the first place, but then she made me wait while she tried on a bra and left me standing outside the dressing room. It was positively frightening!"

Shane stopped snickering long enough to ask, "So you hightailed it when she was in the dressing room?"

"You bet your ass I did!"

"James Wyatt Killian!"

Jamie winced as his sister's voice reached them. Gray and Shane laughed even harder.

Julia stomped up to them and grabbed Jamie by an ear. Jamie squeaked and looked at Gray pleadingly. "Arrest her for assault!" Shane practically had tears in his eyes by this time and Gray couldn't catch his breath, he was so amused.

"He can't arrest me. He isn't in uniform and he's out of his jurisdiction!" Julia smiled at Shane. "Hi, Mr. Cortez." She glared at Gray. "Don't even think about arresting me, Gray!" She pointed a finger in Jamie's face and tugged on his ear harder. "I can't believe you did that! You deserted me!"

"Well, you deserted me first. That bald biker waggled his eyebrows at me, and the chick with the huge ta-tas tried to grope me!" Jamie didn't exactly whine, but it was a close thing.

Julia sighed heavily and shook her head, finally letting go of her younger brother. "Bye, Gray. Bye, Mr. Cortez."

Shane and Gray gasped their farewells in unison, both holding onto their bellies.

"His name is Shane, and he's not that much older than you," Jamie grumbled.

Julia rolled her eyes and shoved him in the back. "Bye, y'all."

Gray and Shane looked at each other and burst into open laughter again as Julia pushed her much larger but younger brother, directing him back to the lingerie store.

"Oh, man! I'm so glad I don't have a sister!"

Shane nodded. "Sisters can be tedious, I'll give you that."

Gray sobered. Shane never talked about his family. In all the years Gray had known him, he never mentioned them. All Gray knew was that Shane had been kicked out of his home when he was sixteen and he'd ended up in Texas. "You have a sister?"

Shane's smile faded. "I used to."

Gray hadn't thought too much on Shane's past. It had never mattered. But now…it still didn't matter, but Gray was curious. "You do?"

"Yeah. Come on, let's go find something for your dad and grab a bite to eat."

Gray hesitated a moment, debating whether he should continue to ask questions. What was the worse Shane could do? Get mad and not talk to him? He was certain he could kiss the man out of the sulks. "What's her name?"

"Sarah."

"Is she older or younger than you?"

"Younger." Shane's voice was getting more and more clipped as he answered.

He knew he was pushing his luck, but Gray couldn't help himself. "Do you have any brothers?"

"No. It was just me and Sarah."

"Why haven't you kept in contact with --"

"Gray." Shane stopped to stare at him, face hard and remote. "I don't want to talk about it. Sarah feels the same way my parents do about me. Leave it alone."

Gray sighed. Clearly now wasn't the right time to learn why Shane's parents had kicked out their only son and eldest child, but he could afford to be patient. Shane wasn't going anywhere and neither was he. He grabbed Shane's hand and squeezed, then let go. "Sorry, Chief."

Shane nodded. After a few more seconds, he grinned. "It's okay. I have a great family now. In fact, we need to hurry, so we can go see them at the hospital."

* * *

Shane hadn't even gotten his key in the lock when Gray's hand cupped his ass, then slid around and grabbed his dick through his jeans. "Wait until we get in the house."

All his admonishing got him was a grumble, then Gray pushed aside his hair, which Gray had unbraided earlier in the day after they'd left the mall. "Hurry up."

As soon as the door opened, Gray herded him inside and locked it. Shane's back hit the door with a thud as Gray's mouth crashed down on his. The kiss was hard, rough. Gray's hands were everywhere, Shane's chest, waist, crotch, then he grabbed two handfuls of Shane's butt and hauled him up against him. Their cocks pressed into each other and Gray grunted into his mouth.

Shane relaxed and went with the passion. Gray needed and he would give, just as he'd always done when Gray had wanted something.

Gray pulled back, his green eyes glazed. "God, Chief, I've been wanting you all day. Watching you in those tight jeans…your hair swaying over that fine ass…those glasses --" Gray moaned, sounding horny as hell, and dove back into the kiss. Soon his mouth moved down Shane's neck, nipping and licking, stopping to suck every now and again.

Shane hadn't even realized Gray had unfastened his jeans till one of his lover's big hands had shoved his jeans and underwear down. The next thing he knew, Gray's other hand was wrapped around his throbbing cock. Shane bucked up into that tight fist, doing some moaning of his own. "What do you want? Anything you want, love…"

"I want to suck you. To feel you in my mouth." Gray dropped to his knees in front of him.

Shane groaned, his hips bucking toward Gray. Those bright green eyes caught his as Gray guided Shane's prick into his mouth. *Oh, Jesus!* Shane's cock jerked at the sight. His fingers flexed, itching to grab that handsome dark head, but he restrained himself and flattened his palms against the door as Gray began to bob up and down, taking his cock in and in and in. Damn, he was good at this. No gagging, no teasing, he just went for it -- and the man could go so far down.

Gray moaned around his prick, then grabbed Shane's hands, guiding them to his face and coming up for air. "Touch me. Fuck my mouth," Gray whispered against Shane's hip before capturing his prick in his hot wet mouth again. He released Shane's hands and clasped Shane's dick with one hand while the other pushed his jeans further down and cupped his balls.

Shane's fingers tightened in Gray's hair. He watched as Gray engulfed him, his lover making all sorts of needy sounds as he swallowed Shane whole. Incredibly, the man was obviously enjoying himself almost as much as Shane was. The fading sunlight coming through the window glinted off Gray's dark hair, making the red stand out. His lover was beautifully masculine and all grown up. Oh, God, yes, this was *his* Gray.

Shane gripped Gray's head and steadily fucked his mouth, his hips pushing his cock all the way to the back of Gray's throat. Gray didn't seem to mind much; in fact, he appeared to love it. His lusty moans and grunts got louder. One hand tugged on his own balls, the other released Shane's to squeeze the base of his prick. Gray's back stiffened slightly and his groans became low and drawn out, but he didn't stop sucking Shane.

Holy Christ! Gray had actually gotten off by blowing him. "Ah, fuck!" Shane's own climax raced up his spine and spilled out of him. He arched his back against the door, holding Gray's head tight, and shot his come down the back of that strong throat. And, damn, if Gray didn't gulp it all down.

Shane sagged against the door. His knees were so weak he was surprised he was still standing. He felt so boneless and…wonderful, the same way he did every time he and Gray made love. His lover had a mouth like nobody else's and he thanked God for it. Good grief, with lips like that, the man was liable to suck Shane's brains right out one of these days. But what a way to go!

Gray flopped onto his back, panting, his arms spread wide and eyes closed.

Shane slid down the door, landing ungracefully on his butt. "Grayson?" He nudged the man with his foot.

Gray's head turned, lids lifting, a soft smile tugging at his lips. "Yeah?"

"If I'd have known that the sight of me in glasses did this to you…I'd have gotten them years ago."

Chapter Eight

"What do you want for supper tonight?"

Shane tossed the last of the fencing supplies onto the flat bed and pulled one of his gloves off with his teeth. Careful to keep the phone trapped between his shoulder and ear, he bumped his straw cowboy hat back before he used the back of his forearm to wipe the sweat off his forehead. "I don't care. Surprise me. Either that or you could come here and we'll eat at the big house."

"Well, then, you better be prepared for us to be answering all sorts of questions about why I'm there and not sleeping in my own bed."

That much was true. And he didn't want to answer those questions. Not now, and not for a long time coming. "Okay, I'm easy. Just lay off the hamburgers. I'm tired of them." Sweat trickled down under his glasses, making him blink, before it dripped in his eye. Damn, it was hot today. He pulled off his other glove and removed his glasses.

"Yeah, I know exactly how easy you are." Shane could hear the smirk in Gray's voice. "What are you doing, Chief? You should distracted."

"Getting stuff to take out to the south pasture. We're replacing the fence."

Gray chuckled, continuing with patent insincerity. "Oh, damn, I'm really sorry I went back to work and missed out on that."

Shane snorted, smiling at the humor in Gray's voice. "Yeah, you sound it, all right. I could always give everyone the day off and wait until you can come help."

"Uh..."

Shane laughed. "You're safe. The fence can't take the time to wait for you. It has to be done before it falls down. The wood posts are completely rotted in some spots, and the barbed wire is hanging without support. It's definitely seen better days."

"Well, hell, Shane, the thing is only twenty years old."

Shane grinned and put his glasses back on. "Well, hopefully it will last longer this time. About a couple of weeks ago, of all damned things, your dad and I debated the fence posts at dinner. Ted likes the way the wood looks -- Lord, that man is determined -- but I like the durability of metal."

"Yeah? So who won the debate?"

"I picked up the supplies, complete with the new metal posts, the day Ted went to the hospital."

Gray chuckled, then sobered. "How is he today?"

"Weak and grouchy as hell about not being able to do much. Wondering why I haven't been at dinner all week."

"Hmm. What did you tell him?"

"That I've been making his only child feed me after I screw his brains out."

Gray laughed. "Actually, Chief, we've been eating dinner before the fun and games." Shane had been going to Gray's place in town every evening since his lover had gone back to work. The two weeks prior to that, Gray had spent all his time at the Broken H or at the hospital, so they'd seen each other daily going on three weeks now.

A loud clank startled Shane, making him realize he wasn't alone. Fortunately, he hadn't been talking loud enough to be overheard. "Hey, listen. I've got work to do. I'll see you tonight, okay?"

"See you tonight, Chief. I'll make hamburgers."

Shane growled. Gray laughed again, then hung up. Shane chuckled and flipped his phone closed, hooking it back to his belt.

Troy, one of his younger workers, had stacked the posts Shane had tossed into the truck bed. He let out a sigh. "Well, Boss, you want to drive?"

"Sure. Call the men and see if we need anything else before we head back to the south pasture. I don't want to have to make another trip all the way back here if we don't have to. I'll see if Kaitlyn has the sandwiches and lemonade made up. I reckon everyone could use a little break before we replace the rest of that damned fence."

"Will do, boss man." Troy pulled his cell phone out and pushed in a number.

Shane grabbed his own phone as it started ringing. He checked the caller ID, half expecting it to be Gray again. *The big house.*

"Kaitlyn, darlin', you must have read my mind. I was about to give you a buzz. Is our lunch was ready to go?"

"Shane, honey, the lunch is ready, but that's not why I called. I need you here. Jim Kauffman came by and he's spouting off all sorts of foul nonsense about you. Ted is steaming up a storm. I'm afraid if you don't come, he's going to slug the man. Heck, son, I'm darned near ready to pop the man a good one myself."

What the --? He hadn't done squat to the man. Hell, he hadn't seen the man in months, despite the fact he was their nearest neighbor. "He's saying stuff about me?"

"Yeah, Shane, honey. Just hurry up, all right? Ted is yelling and that can't be good for him."

Shane frowned. "All right, Kaitlyn, I'm on my way." He frowned at his phone a moment as he ended the call, then glanced at Troy who was waiting on him in the back of the truck bed.

"Well, Boss? Miz Hunter got our food ready to go? The guys say we don't need anything else."

Shane nodded absently; he needed to get going. Kaitlyn was right about Ted, who really shouldn't be getting all riled up, especially this soon out of the hospital. "Yeah, it's ready. Listen, Troy, Kailtyn needs me up at the house for something. Why don't you head on back and take the supplies, and I'll bring the food when I'm done."

"Gotcha!" Troy tipped his hat and jumped out of the truck bed and into the cab before he took off.

Shane quickly strode to the house. He debated calling Gray but dismissed the notion. He'd just see what was going on and deal with it. More than likely it was something stupid, like their cattle eating grass through the fence or an equally ridiculous complaint. It was unlikely there'd be need for the sheriff to get involved. Well, other than for Shane's pleasure at their good sheriff's company. But Gray was a busy man and Shane would see him tonight when he got done with the evening chores.

Shane opened the back door and heard the shouting immediately; they were coming from Ted's office. He looked around the kitchen as he passed through. Kaitlyn was nowhere in sight, but he saw the large coolers she used to pack the men's lunches just about ready to go. Shane headed toward the raised voices.

Kaitlyn stepped away from the office door as he approached and grabbed his arm, pulling him to the side. "Jim said he had to talk to Ted, then he told us all sorts of rubbish about how you got Sherry Ann pregnant."

"What?!" Shane couldn't have been more stunned if Kaitlyn had punched him in the gut.

The voices in the room stopped completely at the sound of Shane's astonishment.

Kaitlyn flinched. "Exactly. Ted and I both told him it was a lie, but that just made him madder. Sherry Ann is --"

"Shane, Son? You out there?"

"Yes, sir." He leaned down and kissed Kaitlyn's cheek. "Don't fret. I'll set the man straight and send him on his way." He took a deep breath to calm himself. Getting mad wouldn't help to quiet down Ted.

Kaityn nodded and patted his arm. "Go on. I'm going to finish some last bits for the men's lunches."

Shane stepped into the office and three sets of eyes stared at him. Shane looked over to the leather couch where Sherry Ann sat, her hands demurely in her lap.

She caught his gaze and looked away quickly.

Shane frowned and gritted his teeth. Damn it! What in the world did the girl think she would gain from this? He wasn't too concerned about her accusations. He'd never touched the girl, and she sure as hell couldn't prove otherwise, but he didn't take kindly to her and her father coming over here upsetting Ted. "What in the devil is this about?"

Ted growled from behind his desk, then jabbed a finger at Jim Kauffman, who was standing by the corner of Ted's desk. "This...*gentleman* --" Ted dragged out the latter word with an abundance of sarcasm. "-- came here demanding that you marry his daughter." Ted's face was red with anger. "He says --"

"Yes, sir, I heard. Kaitlyn told me." Shane crossed over to Ted, laid his hand on his shoulder, and squeezed gently, willing the man to calm down. "It isn't true. Sherry Ann and I barely know each other, and I doubt we even need to discuss the age difference; it's pretty obvious." Shane looked Kauffman right in the eye, daring him to argue. He faced the girl. "Sherry Ann, what is this about? Is this because I told you I wouldn't go out with you?"

Kauffman bristled as he glared at Shane. "Are you calling my daughter a liar?"

Shane ignored the man and moved to the side so he could catch Sherry Ann's gaze again. "You need to tell your daddy the truth."

She looked down at her hands.

Kauffman stepped closer to the desk, thrusting his finger at Shane's chest. "You are a sorry excuse for a man! Trying to shuck your responsibility --"

"Are *you* calling *my* boy a liar?" Ted tensed, starting to rise but Shane put pressure on his shoulder, holding him in his chair, then patted his back.

"Ted, this is nonsense. You shouldn't be getting upset like this." He gazed at Kauffman's enraged face. "Mr. Kauffman, I'm going to have to ask you to leave."

"Bullshit! This why you ran away from home? You get some other girl pregnant all those years ago --"

Shane clenched his teeth and bit down a reply. He wasn't going to get mad, already he could feel Ted stiffening under his hand again. "Mr. Kauffman, I'm not going to do this with you. You can leave on your own or I will gladly escort you off the Broken H."

Kauffman lunged for Shane over the desk. Shane readied himself to catch the man's fist, but a slow smooth draw from the doorway brought both men to an instant halt.

"I wouldn't do that if I were you, Mr. Kauffman."

Gray. Shane barely suppressed a grin. He flicked a glance past Kauffman, then looked back, not trusting the man enough to let his attention stray for long.

Gray stood in the doorframe, long legs in an open stance. One arm hung by his side; the other was on his hip, above his gun. He was in uniform, tan cowboy hat pulled low over his face, concealing his eyes. "What seems to be the problem?"

Kauffman sputtered and turned to face Gray. "This is none of your concern, sheriff."

Ted started to say something, but Gray shot him a glance and raised his hand. "Well, Mr. Kauffman, last I heard, I *am* part of this family. So explain to me what has you so irate that you felt it was necessary to charge over here and start an argument with my father, who is just out of the hospital?"

Kauffman pointed at Shane without looking at him. "He got my Sherry Ann pregnant and refuses to take responsibility for it."

A frown tugged at Gray's lips. He pushed his hat back and his green eyes met Shane's. He raised a brow, then looked back to Kauffman. "Shane?"

He almost groaned. Shane knew that look; loud and clear, it said, "I told you so."

"Grayson?"

"Did you get this man's daughter in a family way?"

"I most certainly did not. And I already told him that."

"You're done here, Mr. Kauffman. I think you and Sherry Ann need to leave."

Kauffman scoffed, looking like an enraged bull. "I am not done! Sherry Ann is sixteen and underage. I'm filing statutory rape charges."

Ted stood up. "Enough! You get the hell out of my house!"

Shane pushed the older man back down. "Shh... He won't get anywhere because it's not true. There is no sense in you getting upset over this, Ted."

"Everyone stop shouting. We are all in the same room." Gray pushed away from the wall. "Mr. Kauffman, do you have any proof that Shane and your daughter had sex?"

"I don't need proof! Sherry Ann said he's the father of her baby! You're the sheriff, it's your job to arrest him."

"You get me proof, and I'll do that. Now, you are upsetting my parents and Shane. I'm asking you one more time to leave."

Kauffman puffed out his chest.

Gray slowly shook his head. "Mr. Kauffman, if I have to ask again, I'm going to arrest you for trespassing.

Kauffman stood there for several seconds, obviously trying to decide what to do. Finally, Sherry Ann, conspicuously silent throughout the entire exchange, stood and went to her father.

"Come on, Daddy. Let's go."

Jim Kauffman spun back toward Shane, eyes livid. "You will be hearing from my lawyer!" Then he and his daughter quickly left.

Shane, Gray and Ted all stayed silent until they heard the front door slam shut.

"Chief, I told you the girl was trouble. You didn't bother to tell her daddy about the way she's been pestering you, did you?"

Shane felt a smile forming. He liked seeing Gray stand up and take charge. "No, I didn't. He wouldn't have believed me."

Gray acknowledged the truth of that with a nod. "You're right, he wouldn't have, but you still should have brought it up. And a lot sooner, I might add. If you'd had a heart-to-heart with him earlier, this fiasco might have been avoided. Since you didn't file a restraining order on her, I couldn't do anything about it anyway. You gonna listen to me and file on her now? You better hope she doesn't just decide that if she can't have you, no one can, and shoots your ass."

Shane groaned. "Listen, the kid is just mixed up. She'll come clean, you'll see. She's just trying to get attention, is all." He knew damned well how badly it hurt to have one's parents turn their backs on a child, and that was essentially what Kauffman did off and on to Sherry Ann. The kid was just trying to get her father to notice her any way she could. She'd likely 'fess up in a day or so and tell him it was all a lie.

Ted looked at Shane. "This girl been giving you problems, boy?"

"She's been bothering him, Dad." Gray sat down on the couch.

Shane moved to the chair in front of Ted's desk and seated himself. "She's harmless."

Ted raised a brow. "Lying and saying you got her knocked up is harmless?"

Gray's radio went off, interrupting their discussion. "Shit!" He informed the dispatcher he was on his way, then focused his attention on Shane again. "We are going to have a long talk about this, Chief. I know you feel sorry for her, but this behavior of hers has got to be dealt with. God only knows what she's going to do next." He stood. "Daddy, you all right?"

Right on cue, Kaitlyn came bustling in, immediately fussing over her husband. "He will be."

"Good."

His mother smiled. "Thank you for coming, baby."

"Thanks for calling me, Mama. I'm glad I wasn't too far away. If he comes back, I expect you to let me know. I'd hate for Shane to get to do all the ass-kicking by himself. That wouldn't be fair." He winked at Shane and smiled broadly.

Shane rolled his eyes. "I had it under control."

Gray snorted. "So I saw. Very impressive self-control. I'd've been spitting mad, myself."

"Well, I know it isn't true."

Kaitlyn stopped rubbing Ted's shoulders long enough to pat Shane's arm. "We all know it isn't true, Shane."

Gray and Shane shared a smile, then Gray frowned. "Now you have both him and Sherry Ann to deal with. That man is spiteful as hell; he's not going to let this go. I have no doubt he's going to drag you through the dirt, Chief. He's going to dig up stuff you'd probably rather he didn't."

Shane's stomach sank a little. He suspected that Gray was going to be proven right.

Chapter Nine

Shane stood outside the big house more nervous than he'd ever been in his life. He sat down on the back porch swing and dropped his head in his hands, knocking his hat off. It was still an hour before Gray got off work.

He wanted to go next door and strangle Sherry Ann. He could understood to an extent why the girl was doing this, but Gray was right: Kauffman wasn't the kind of man to let go of a perceived insult to his inflated sense of self. In this case, it would appear his daughter's honor, or lack thereof, was tied to his own.

Shane sighed; he was partly to blame for not having put a stop to Sherry Ann's nonsense sooner. Shane hadn't really considered the ramifications of Kauffman's tenacity and bullheadedness until Gray had pointed them out. If he dug in the right places, it wouldn't be hard for the man to discover Shane's homosexuality. Shane had been very careful to hide it, but it wasn't like no one else knew.

He wasn't concerned about what most people thought of him, but the Hunters were his family. They deserved to know and should hear it from him, not the town gossips. God, he did not want to do this.

The back door opened. "Shane? Honey, you all right?" Kaitlyn bent and picked up Shane's hat, then sat down on the swing next to him.

Shane turned his head to look at her and she handed him his hat. "Thank you." He put it back on his head and leaned back in the swing.

"You're welcome. What's the matter, Shane? And don't tell me nothing. I've known you a long time and I darn well know when something is bothering you." She reached out and rubbed his back. "Is it this nonsense with Sherry Ann? Honey, don't worry about that. We all know you don't have anything going with that little girl. The child needs her backside blistered."

Shane nodded and closed his eyes. She sure did, and at this point Shane was considering being first in line to volunteer to administer it. Kaitlyn was like a mother to him, always trying to take care of him. She treated him damned near the way she treated Gray. He opened his eyes and took her hand, lightly squeezing. "Kaitlyn, I...thank you. Thank you for being the mother that mine never was. I could never repay all that you've done for me over the years. No matter what happens, I want you to know that and that I love you."

Kaitlyn framed his face with her hands, pulling him down to kiss his forehead. "I love you, too, honey. Nothing going to change that. You are like a son to me; you have been for a long, long time. Taking you in was never a hardship, you know. You've always been very appreciative and you've repaid us in kind over and over. Try not to be so upset over this. It will work out, I promise."

He hoped like hell that she was right -- and that she still felt the same way after he told them what he needed to say. "Ted still awake?"

"He's in his office. You eating with us tonight?"

Shane got up, drawing Kaitlyn with him. "I actually have plans for dinner tonight, but I'd like to talk to the two of you first."

Kaitlyn gave him a speculative look, opened her mouth to say something, then closed it. "Come on in, then." She tugged him behind her into the house. When they reached the office, Shane had the sudden urge to flee.

"Ted, Shane has something he wants to talk to us about." Kaitlyn let go of his hand and went to the couch and sat down.

"Oh, good, I have something I want to talk to him about, too." Ted glanced up from some papers on his desk and smiled at Shane.

Shane swallowed hard and took a deep breath. He pulled his hat off, circling it around and around in his hands.

Ted looked at Shane's hands and frowned, then gazed back to meet his eyes. "I'm guessing this is pretty serious. Have a seat, son. You aren't going to tell me that you *did* get that Kauffman girl pregnant are you?"

"No! Oh, good Lord, no!"

Ted grinned. "Well, I didn't think so, but you look like you're going to a funeral."

Shane walked across the office and sat down beside Kaitlyn.

"I...Gray was right today when he said that Kauffman was probably going to dig up a lot of stuff about me. And I owe the two of you too much to not let y'all know what he's likely to find out." *Damn, this sucks!* His stomach was such a mess he wasn't going to be able to eat a damned thing tonight. He had the sudden urge to throw up.

Kaitlyn patted his knee encouragingly.

Ted nodded. "This have anything to do with why you left New Mexico at alone at sixteen and ended up in Texas?"

Shane nodded. "Sort of."

"Well, I can't tell you that we haven't wondered over the years, but I'll be honest, son, I doubt you can tell me anything that is going to make me think less of you. I've watched you grow up, boy, I know what kind of man you are. Whatever you ran from, was a long time ago and --"

"I'm gay!" *Well, shit!* He'd just blurted that right out, hadn't he?

Ted sat still for several seconds, frowning, eyebrows pulled together.

Kaitlyn gasped, clutched her hands to her chest and flopped back against the couch. "Oh, God!"

Shane felt tears burning his eyes. He couldn't look at either one of the Hunters. They didn't understand and were going to toss him out. Worse, they didn't love him anymore.

Kaitlyn took a deep breath and dropped her head in her hands. "Oh, God, honey! You scared the heck out of me! I thought you were going tell us you'd murdered someone."

What?! Shane's mouth dropped open.

Ted groaned. "Now, Katy, how it the world could you think that?"

His wife blushed. "Well, what did *you* think he was going to say?"

"I thought maybe he'd stolen a car or something."

Shane couldn't help himself; he just stared, looking back and forth between the two of them. He didn't know whether to be insulted or relieved. They'd thought he was a criminal on the lam? Did this mean they didn't care that he was gay?

Kaitlyn wrapped her arms around Shane, hugging him tightly. "Honey, you look like you've seen a ghost. Say something."

"Y'all don't care?"

Ted chuckled. "Hell, son, we've known that for years!"

Shane was aghast. "You have?"

Kaitlyn nodded. "Of course, honey. Is that why you left home so young?"

Even after all this time and in the midst of one of the hardest conversations he'd ever had, Shane still felt old anger boiling up inside him. He clenched his jaw and gave a crisp nod, hoping like hell the response would be enough.

Ted got up from his chair and slowly made his way around the desk and over to the couch. He sat down on Shane's other side and slung an arm over his shoulder. "We figured as much. You don't have to talk about it. Nothing has changed, son. We love and support you, just like always."

Shane swallowed hard. "How long have you known?" Did he dare to ask how they'd known?

"Since you were a teen, honey. You never brought it up, so neither did we." Kaitlyn reached behind him, grabbing Ted's hand.

Shane felt a tear slip down and swiped a finger under his glasses to catch it. It felt like a huge weight had been lifted off his chest. Ted and Kaitlyn hugged him and each other.

Kaitlyn kissed his cheek. "Did I tell you I like the glasses?"

Shane grinned and shook his head. "No, but thank you."

"So when do we get to meet him, boy?"

Huh? Shane jerked his head around to face Ted.

"You're seeing someone, aren't you? That's why you aren't eating at home and why you've told us not to wait up for you, isn't it?"

Oh, shit! How in the hell did he answer that without telling them about Gray? Shane silently groaned. Oh, man, he'd solved one problem only to realize he had another. He had no idea how they'd react to him seeing Gray. Would they think he'd taken advantage of Gray? Probably not, they weren't those kinds of people. They truly cared for him, but he was so tired of emotionally draining confessions today. And what if it got out that Gray was gay? How would that affect him in the community? At work? Shane didn't care so much what others thought of him or how they treated him, but Gray... He didn't want to chance it, not now, and it wasn't up to him to tell them before Gray did. Or, at the very least, the two of them tell his parents together.

Ted chuckled. "Well, hell, boy, you don't have to bring him home. You look like a teen balking at bringing your prom date to meet your folks."

Shane chuckled. "It's not that. I just...well, I'll talk to him, see if he wants to come to dinner one night."

Kaitlyn grinned. "Good. We miss not having you eat with us. It's bad enough that Gray doesn't come by more often. Although I will point out that you are way too late. You should have done this years ago when most kids bring their girlfriends or boyfriends home to meet their parents." Kaitlyn rose. "I'm going to go start dinner." She stood in front of Shane and patted his head. "We love you, honey. You don't have to be afraid to tell us stuff; you should know that by now."

Shane got up and hugged her tightly, warmth welling up in his chest. "Love you, too…Mom."

When he pulled back, Kaitlyn had tears in her eyes. "I like that! You call me that anytime you want. I'll always answer, you hear?" She pinched his cheek, gave him a watery smile and left the room.

Ted left the couch and slapped Shane on the back. "Get out of here, boy! Go meet your date."

Shane grinned and put his hat back on his head. "Yes, sir." He turned to leave, but Ted's voice brought him up short. "Son, if Kauffman starts anything else, I want to know. I've already talked to our lawyer, and he's working on it, but it's gonna take time. If nothing else we can get them for slander."

"I just want them to buzz off."

Ted nodded. "I imagine we can do that, too." He was quiet for a moment, then smiled. "And, Shane?"

Shane faced Ted.

"I'm happy that you've finally found someone important enough to get you off the Broken H now and again."

I just hope you still feel that way, when you find out that someone is your son.

Gray had just finished filling the tea pitcher with water when he heard the door open. He grinned and pulled down two glasses. "You're just in time; the hamburgers are almost done."

Shane groaned from the living room. "If you're serious, I'm going to beat you, then hightail out of here!"

Gray chuckled as he filled his and Shane's glasses with ice and tea. "Nah, of course I'm not serious -- we're actually having hot dogs."

Shane's groan was closer this time, almost behind him, in fact. "I'm still going to beat you."

"I'm joking, Chief. I ordered pizza. I got home late and --" Gray swung around and stopped dead in his tracks.

Shane stood a little way inside the kitchen sporting a pair of low-slung jeans and a red pullover with a collar. The clothes were nice, but that wasn't what had garnered Gray's attention. Shane's hair was loose and hanging down his back, slightly damp from the looks of it.

"Damn! I...you...damn!" Gray wordlessly held out the tea. His cock had already started to fill. After Shane took the refreshment, Gray reached down and adjusted himself.

Shane's lips quirked. "Hmm, must be my sexy eyewear again. Thanks for the tea."

Gray looked at the gold wire-rimmed frames and hell if his prick didn't get even harder. He sighed and shook his head. "Yeah, they're pretty hot, but I was drooling over your hair." He tipped his head toward the little, round, four-seater table in the middle of the kitchen. "Have a seat. I'll get us some plates and napkins."

Shane did so and lifted his nose, sniffing. "Mmm...pepperoni, hamburger, sausage and jalapeños. You remembered." He took another whiff of the air, then settled back. "I broke my rubber band on the way out the door and didn't want to go back for another one. You'd think I'd learn to keep a bunch stashed in my truck."

Gray chuckled, grabbing two plates and some paper towels off the roll next to the sink, then opened the oven door and removed some pizza slices. "Not that I'm complaining, but if you wouldn't continue to try and wrap the things around again after you've stretched them to their limits, you wouldn't keep snapping them." He handed Shane a plate and watched the man dig in.

"Yeah, but if I don't get them tight enough, my hair slips out. Then what would be the point?" Shane took a bite. "Mmm..."

Gray munched on a slice himself. "How did things go after I left today? Kauffman didn't come back, did he?"

Shane shrugged and finished chewing his pizza. "No; things were fine. I left right after you to get back out to the south pasture and put up the new fence." He paused to take another bite. "You know, I don't get it. What does Sherry Ann possibly think to gain by this? Does she think if she can trap me that I'll somehow magically fall head over heels in love with her and marry her?"

"I don't know, Chief. The whole thing is weird."

Shane grunted his agreement.

"She's obviously got problems if she'd make up such a story to get revenge on you. And I want you to file a restraining order against both her and Kauffman. She needs to stay the hell away from you and I want him to keep his distance, too." He lifted his eyes to let Shane know he meant it. "You think she really is pregnant?"

"Who knows? But if she is, it sure as hell isn't mine."

Gray snorted. "It's quite possible she's really pregnant and doesn't want to tell her daddy who the baby's father is."

Shane shrugged. "Maybe so, but I can't see how pointing the finger at me is going to help anything. I think she's still trying to get her father's notice, albeit in a somewhat extreme way. You think I should try and talk to her by herself, see what the hell she's thinks she's doing?"

Gray had started shaking his head before Shane finished talking. "No. Stay as far away from her as possible. I don't need people telling me they've seen you together and her hollering rape or something. That girl obviously has issues, I wouldn't put that past her. Not to mention you might agitate things by confronting her. At this point, they have to prove that she's, one, pregnant and, two, if she is that you're the father. And they can't. They definitely won't have DNA evidence of any sexual activity, and if she's with child, it's much too soon to get DNA results from the fetus."

"Yeah, okay. I'll keep away from them, but there isn't any need to file for a restraining order."

Gray groaned.

"I'm tired of talking about the Kauffmans, so let's drop it. Besides, I need to discuss something else."

Gray frowned, letting him know the business of the restraining order wasn't done. "Oh?"

Shane nodded. "Yeah, but not now. Eat."

He studied Shane for a few minutes, trying to decide whether to push or not. Shane didn't look visibly upset, so he decided that whatever it was would wait. They sat in silence, taking care of four slices of pizza apiece. Finally, Gray pushed away from the table a little and leaned back, relaxed. "You staying the night?"

Shane nodded. "I will if you'll set the alarm for five."

"As long as you don't expect me to get up that early."

Shane chuckled and moved back from the table, too. "Lazy."

Gray nodded. "Yup, that's why I went into law enforcement instead of ranching. No getting up with the roosters for me. It isn't natural to be up before the sun is." He grabbed his plate and reached for Shane's. "You done?"

"Yeah, thanks. I really was tired of hamburgers."

"I was, too, and would have made something but that last call took more time than I thought, so I didn't get back into the office till way after my shift ended. And I'm off this weekend." He put the plates in the sink and came back to Shane. He dropped to his knees in front of his lover, resting his hands on the man's thighs. "I'll fix something tomorrow. Maybe we can do something like fishing or go into San Antonio for a movie."

Shane shifted in his chair, spreading his legs wider. He looked down at Gray and grinned. "We could do that. Next weekend I'm going to a livestock auction. Want come with me? If you're especially nice, I'll buy you a horse. Only you have to break it in."

"Sure. Do I get to ride on your shoulders like when I was a kid?"

"I'll give you something to ride…"

Gray ran his hands up and down Shane's denim-clad thighs. His gaze drifted down Shane's long body, finally settling on the bulge in his jeans. The sight made his own cock stand up and take notice. He unbuttoned and unzipped Shane's pants, tugging the flaps apart. "Mmm, and what a nice ride it's going to be." He hooked his fingers beneath the waistband of the jeans and Shane's underwear.

Shane lifted his hips just a little, allowing Gray to tug them down to mid-thigh. The beautiful wide prick that gave so much pleasure came free. It wasn't hard yet, but it was getting there. Shane's hand traced down the side of Gray's cheek, his thumb rubbing back and forth over the cheekbone.

Gray looked into the brown eyes, taking a minute to absorb the beauty of that beloved face. Damn, those glasses really were sexy. Maybe Shane would let him --

"What are you thinking?" Shane smiled quizzically.

"Why?"

"You've suddenly got this naughty little glint in your eyes."

Gray inspected Shane's lap, noticing the now fully erect cock. He touched it and squeezed gently, making Shane hiss out a breath. "Just thinking about those glasses."

"No."

"You don't even know what I want to do. Please?" He swiped his tongue up the long shaft along the prominent vein.

Shane groaned and scooted his ass closer to the edge of the chair. "You aren't spunking on my glasses, you perv."

Gray twirled his tongue around the plump head, sucking it deeper into his mouth. His own dick was like a brand inside his uniform trousers. He unfastened them as he gulped Shane further down his throat, then pulled back up. "Come on, Chief. Haven't you ever watched porn? The guy with the glasses always gets --"

Shane gripped his cock and tapped the head against Gray's lips. Obediently, he opened his mouth again and engulfed Shane, forgetting all about what he was saying. He *was* going to come on those glasses and that fucking beautiful face, but he'd argue his case later.

When Shane's hands wrapped around his head, he swore his own prick leaked copiously. Oh, man, he loved that. There was just something that turned him on to no end about having Shane's hands on his skull while Gray sucked him off. The idea that Shane was so desperate for him that he didn't want him to stop, that he needed to hold his head there, was a huge turn on. He'd always loved sucking dick -- he had a bit of an oral fixation, truth be told -- but the fact that it was Shane...

He'd never been able to get off just from giving head before -- well, aside from the first time he'd ever done it -- but with Chief it was becoming the norm. In fact, if Shane started thrusting, he was a goner. The very idea that he could make Shane lose control just about did him in every time.

Now, if he could just get the man to talk dirty to him, he'd be set.

He began to stroke himself as he bobbed his head up and down on Shane's prick, sucking every time his mouth slid up. Shane groaned, his hands caressing Gray's head, then he started moving, thrusting up as his hands pushed Gray's head down. Shane already knew that Gray could not only take it, but loved it when he did that.

Gray opened up, relaxing his throat muscles. He sat back on his heels and used his hand to push Shane's cock down so he could get a better angle, allowing Shane's penis to slip all the way down. He could feel the blood throbbing in his own dick and the slick precome dribbling out the tip. His balls were so tight, so close to emptying.

The sounds of Shane's rough breathing and the slick sounds of his own saliva and the suction of his mouth sounded loud in the quiet room. "Oh, damn, Grayson. That's it. Take all of it."

The hoarse whisper was all Gray needed. He shot hard, groaning around Shane's dick. Come squirted out, slicking his fingers and splattering on the floor. The whole time he continued to suck, never slowing in his quest to pleasure Shane.

Shane bucked up into his mouth several more times, then tensed. His fingers flexed in Gray's hair and he gasped something that sounded like, "Grayson, love, now," and came. The salty flavor poured into Gray's mouth and down his throat as he swallowed.

Gray slumped a little, trying to recover from his own orgasm, but kept Shane's prick in his mouth. He sucked and licked, reluctant to let go, enjoying the weight of Shane's softening prick in his mouth.

Shane chuckled and caressed his cheek. "That almost tickles."

"Ummm…"

Shane laughed outright. "*That* does tickle."

Gray smiled, letting Shane slip from his mouth. He kissed Shane's thigh and rested his head on Shane's knee.

"You really love doing that, don't you?" Shane combed his fingers through Gray's hair.

He nodded. "Yeah, I do. Especially with you."

Shane caught his head in his big tanned hands and pulled Gray up, urging him onto his knees. Once Gray was face level, Shane leaned forward and kissed him, his tongue softly caressing, exploring. It wasn't a deep or passionate kiss -- it was soft and sweet and lazy, with just a hint of tongue -- but it spoke volumes. Shane pulled back, his gaze tracing slowly over Gray's face, a soft smile on his lips. "I told your parents today that I'm gay."

"Yeah?"

"Yeah. They said they already knew." Shane frowned at the memory.

Gray grinned. "Well, hell, Chief, they've known you since you were sixteen. If they hadn't had at least an inkling, I'd have to wonder. I'm sure they know about me, too."

"Well, you didn't know I was."

"Yeah, but I had reason to believe otherwise."

Shane shrugged. "I didn't mention you, but they know I'm seeing someone. I've been told that I should bring you home to meet them."

Gray chuckled. "You could have told them. I wouldn't have cared." He knew they'd all deal with it. He had great parents. Heck, he would have told them years ago if he hadn't been worried about what Shane would say. Ironically, telling them now wasn't a big deal since he knew he wouldn't have Shane's censure to deal with.

Shane shook his head. "It's not my place. You need to tell them." His brows drew together.

Gray smoothed the lines. "You're worried about what they will think? About us together, I mean?"

Shane gave a crisp nod.

"You want me to tell them? I can do it tomorrow."

"No!"

Gray started. "Okay."

"I'm sorry, I just need a little time. They need a little more time. They've had a lot to deal with lately, what with Ted's heart attack, then the Kauffmans and their lame-ass accusation, then me telling them I'm gay. Maybe we should wait a while."

Gray didn't think it was that big a deal, but obviously it meant something to Shane, so he could hold off on telling his folks. "Yeah, we can wait as long as you want, but I don't think it will matter. Well, they might be a little surprised at first, but they love us. They'll be happy."

Shane leaned forward and kissed him again. Just a soft brush of lips. "God, I hope you're right."

Chapter Ten

Maybe he could just do like he did as a kid: open the back door and shout, "I'm at Shane's!" Back in the day, no one would have raised a brow. It would be so much simpler if he could tell them the truth, but he'd promised Shane to give him time.

Gray blew out a deep breath. By the time he rounded the second of the four curves on the way to the Broken H, he still hadn't decided what he was going to tell his parents -- or rather how not to tell them until Shane was ready to do so.

Gray wasn't sure why exactly, but he had a feeling Shane needed to work out something for himself.

Around the third curve, he spotted riders on the edge of the Broken H's property. As he got closer, he realized it was Shane with Mac, one of the older ranch hands. Mac had worked on the Broken H since Gray was a kid. The man used to stay up at the bunkhouse, but he'd gotten married close to fifteen years ago and move to his own house in town. He was a nice guy, closer to Shane's age than Gray's.

Shane saw him and waved. He waved back, pulled over to the side of the dirt road, killed the engine and waited.

Shane and Mac veered toward the fence, coming to meet him.

Gray hopped out, heading toward the two men. "Hey, Chief! Hey, Mac!"

"Hey, sheriff!" Mac smiled.

"Grayson." Shane tipped his straw cowboy hat.

Gray stopped next to the fence, petting Kokopelli, Shane's black gelding, on the white star above his nose. "What are y'all doing out this far?"

Mac grinned. "As little as possible. Ahem, I mean, we're riding the fence."

Shane shrugged, grinning. "You're off work early."

Gray nodded. "Sure am. I got out of there an hour earlier than I expected. I'd already packed a bag before I left, so I came right here. How's Daddy today?"

Mac let out a long whistle. "Grouchy as hell!"

Gray laughed. "In that case, I'm in no hurry. How about you, Mac? You want to trade me? Take my truck back to the ranch and let me ride Dixie back?"

Mac's face lit up, then he looked over at Shane.

Shane nodded. "Sure, go ahead. You can go home when you get there."

"Thanks, Shane." Mac got off the chestnut mare and climbed through the fence.

Gray tossed him the keys to his truck. "Just park it out behind the big house and leave the keys in it."

Mac caught the key ring from the air and smiled. "Will do! Later, Shane. Later, Gray!"

Gray climbed between the barbed wire, nearly knocking his tan hat off, then mounted. He glanced at Shane. "Let's go."

Mac honked and saluted them as he drove off.

"How long has it been since you've been on a horse?"

"About a year. Why?"

Shane grinned. "Well, since you somehow managed to stay off one while you were out here helping the last two weeks, I was just trying to get an idea of how sore you're going to be."

Gray snorted. "I stayed off the horses so I could stay close to the foreman's cottage and ride you instead. Besides, it's like riding a bike." He gave Shane a heated look.

Shane chuckled, turning the black quarter horse around so that he was facing the big house. "Be nice and I'll message your thighs and ass for you tonight."

"I'm counting on it. And maybe afterward we could --" His gaze flicked down and back to Shane's eyes, or rather his glasses.

"No." Shane started Koko moving again.

Gray turned Dixie and caught up to him. "You don't even know what I was going to say."

"Does it have to do with my glasses?"

Damn! Gray groaned. "Fine."

Shane smiled. "You have any other perversions I should know about?"

"Is that a trick question?" Gray studied Shane for a minute. Damn, the man looked fine on a horse.

"Why would that be a trick question?"

"'Cause I've always had a thing for your hair." What would that long mane feel like wrapped around his --

Shane laughed. "Oh, no."

"No?" Gray grinned so wide his face hurt. God, this was fun.

"No, you aren't jerking off in my hair." Shane was still chuckling.

"How 'bout using it to wrap around my dick while I --"

Shane shook his head and snorted loudly. "No. Geez, I had no idea you had all these fetishes."

"What can I say, Chief, you inspire me." And he did, too. Gray had never really considered himself kinky. But, man, he sure did want to try out a few things with Shane. He peered down at the cuffs on his belt. Gray shivered, his cock hardening right up.

"What was that about? That little moan?"

Moan? He'd moaned? "Just thinking about you cuffing me to the bed."

Shane turned, meeting him eye to eye, serious as could be. "Now, that I could do." That intense stare made Gray's cock stiffen further. He swept a glance down Shane's body.

Shane adjusted himself, facing forward. "You ever done that? Let someone tie you up?"

"Nope. Never trusted anyone enough." And that was the truth; the thought of it with any other lover would have scared the hell out him.

Shane groaned. "Damn!" He rearranged his dick again. "Change the subject already. How was work?"

Good idea. Gray shifted in the saddle, making Dixie side step a little. "Work was good. Slow as usual. Not that I'm complaining. It beats getting shot at like the time I was on the force in San Antone."

Shane's jaw tightened. "Yeah, definitely better."

The realization that Shane had worried about him should have made him feel good, but it didn't. He'd never considered that his former job scared Shane, but he supposed he should have. He didn't like the thought of Shane being uneasy because of him. Shane had been there with Gray's parents the day he'd been shot. It had only been a flesh wound, but all three of them had showed up on the door step of his apartment mere hours after they'd heard. They had to have left the ranch immediately to have gotten there as quickly as they did.

"It's better than you riding bulls, too."

"You never said anything. You never told me it bothered you."

"You weren't speaking to me at the time." Shane gave him a meaningful look, then abruptly grinned. "I used to get nauseous when I saw you ride."

"You watched me on the circuit?" He couldn't remember ever seeing Shane at a rodeo. Of course, if Shane had been in the stands and stayed away, he wouldn't have.

"Several times. I was there the night you came off that bull and hit the gate, knocking yourself unconscious." Shane sat straighter in the saddle, his jaw tightening again. "I like you being sheriff."

Damn! That had been a fucked up night. Later, Gray thought he'd seen Shane stay with him in the hospital, but he'd convinced himself that it was a hallucination from his concussion. "I'm sorry I worried you, Chief." A little quieter, he added, "Thank you for sitting with me all night."

Shane's eyes shot to his, surprised.

"I thought I was seeing things."

Shane nodded once, his demeanor still stiff, but slowly relaxing.

It was time to change the subject again, but first…"I like me being sheriff, too."

Shane smiled. His eyes raked down Gray, then up. The stare was so intense that if Gray didn't know better, he'd have thought Shane could see through his uniform. Shane moved on the saddle and looked away.

"So, what am I going to tell my parents?"

"I told them you were coming out to help with chores this morning. I also told your mom we'd both be eating dinner with them."

"I know, but aren't they going to wonder why I'm sleeping at your place?"

"Nope. I told them that I'd put you up at my place, so you wouldn't be going in and out disturbing them."

"That worked?"

"Yup, 'cause then I remembered something I had to do and rushed out, before they could assure me you wouldn't disturb them."

Gray laughed. Well, that was one way to handle it. He still thought it would be easier to just tell them. That way they'd quite bugging Shane to meet his boyfriend and everything would be out in the open, but he wasn't going to pressure Shane.

"Come on. I need a shower before dinner. And if we hurry, I might have enough time to cuff you to the bed before we have to go eat." Shane and Koko took off in a gallop.

Gray choked back a laugh and heeled his horse. So much for his thighs and backside not being sore; his cock had decided to give chase.

* * *

"Really, honey, you won't be disturbing us if you want to stay here." Kaitlyn bussed Gray as she handed him a plate of cookies.

"It's okay, Mom. I'm going to get up early with Shane tomorrow and feed the animals and stuff. Maybe go fishing." Gray kissed his mother back and opened the kitchen door.

Shane snagged a chocolate chip cookie off the plate Gray was holding on his way out the door. Gray grumbled playfully and pulled the plate closer to his body. "I got these for me."

"Don't be greedy, or I won't take you fishing tomorrow." Shane took a bite of cookie, making sure to "Mmm" loudly.

Kaitlyn chuckled. "Should I fix you your own plate of goodies, Shane?"

He kissed Kaitlyn's cheek. "Nope, I'm good. Thank you for dinner. Call if you need anything."

"I will." She returned Shane's kiss and whispered, "I'm so glad the two of you are getting along again."

Shane felt a stab of guilt but managed a grin and a wink. "Me, too." He popped the rest of the cookie in his mouth and stepped onto the porch, leaving Gray to follow. "Night, Kaitlyn."

"Night, Shane. I'll fix breakfast at six tomorrow if you boys are interested."

"We'll be here, Mom. Night."

"Night, Gray."

The back door clicked shut and Gray caught up to him, halfway across the drive. "They seemed happy to have us both at dinner."

"Yeah, they did. It's been a long time since we've both been there, with the exception of Thanksgiving and Christmas. They've missed you, and you're probably the best medicine possible for your dad. He looked better tonight. More color in his face, did you notice?"

Gray moved beside him, offering him a cookie. "Yes, I did."

Shane accepted it, popping it into his mouth as he swung open the front door of his home. Gray strolled in past him, stuffing another cookie in his own mouth, looking happy and carefree.

Shane grinned and shut and locked the door. He finished off his cookie and followed Gray into the kitchen. After Gray dumped the remaining cookies into the cookie jar on counter, Shane took the plate from him and placed it in the sink. He twined both arms around Gray's neck and kissed his chin. "Go to the bedroom, get naked and I'll be right there."

Gray's lip lifted on one side. He opened his mouth to say something, but Shane silenced him with a finger on his lips.

"Shh. Go."

Gray's eyes twinkled, then he turned and hightailed it to the bedroom so quickly Shane couldn't help but chuckle.

As soon as Gray was out of sight and rustling from the bedroom signaled he was getting undressed, Shane went to the closet next to the front door. Unfortunately, they'd had to hurry to dinner and hadn't gotten to play earlier, but he was pretty sure there was some rope in there.

He'd never given much thought to tying anyone up, but after Grayson had mentioned it this afternoon, the idea had taken root and refused to let go. A chance to worship that magnificent body without Gray touching back and making him insane with those incredible hands and mouth was very appealing. All throughout dinner he'd sat there, alternately conversing and eating while imagining Gray naked and cuffed to his bed. He'd had a hell of a time not reaching under the table and repositioning his hard on during dinner. His prick was rock hard just thinking about tying Gray up.

Shane rummaged through the junk, a lawn chair, a baseball bat, a tent...good grief he needed to go through this closet. *Aha!* He pulled out a coil of nylon rope. This would work much better than cuffs. He put all the other stuff back, closed the door and headed for the bedroom.

Gray was stretched out naked on the big four-poster, his long legs slightly spread and his hands behind his head. His cock was hard, arched slightly over his defined belly. His abs and pectoral muscles quivered, flexing when he saw Shane. Shane's own cock was fully erect. He unsnapped and unzipped his jeans, giving himself more room.

Gray grinned, examining him closely. When he noticed the rope, he got a gleam in his eye. "Thought you were going to use my cuffs, Chief."

Shane shook his head, coming close to the bed. "They'd hurt your wrists. 'Sides this way I can tie your legs, too." He tossed the coil on to the bed next to Gray and opened the nightstand drawer, looking for a pocket knife. He pulled out the lube and tossed it next to the rope and continued to dig. Finally, he found what he was looking for; Gray had given it to him as a gift one Christmas.

"You're going to tie my legs, too?" Gray's brow furrowed and his body tensed a little.

Shane sat down on the edge of the bed and ran his fingers over Gray's stomach, feeling the muscles jump under his attention. He caught Gray's gaze. "Not if you don't want me to."

Gray thought about it for a minute. His body seemed to loosen up and he came upright, reaching for Shane. Shane pulled him close, pressing their lips together, trying to reassure him. But Gray turned the tables on him and took over their kiss. His tongue caressed and laved the inside of Shane's mouth, pushing in and out. Shane moaned and pulled away. The idea was to pleasure Gray, not to get immersed himself. "Can I tie you up, Grayson?"

Gray nodded, his eyes half closed and smoldering. He reached for Shane again. "Come 'ere first, Chief."

Shane shook his head and deflected his lover's hands. "Lie down and spread your arms and legs so I can tie them to the posts."

Gray grumbled something that sounded like, "Meanie" but did as Shane directed.

Shane made quick work of cutting the rope into four equal sections and securing Gray's limbs to the big wooden bed frame. He tied them loosely so that Gray could get free if he really wanted to and so the rope wouldn't cut into his skin. He wanted Gray in ecstasy, not pain. He stepped back, looking at his handy work and nearly swallowed his tongue.

His randy sheriff was already panting, a small sheen of sweat over his body, and his skin was pale against the dark blue comforter. His eyes were shut now, his bottom lip caught between his teeth. Those firm stomach muscles flexed and his hips lifted off the bed, making his dick bob -- a glistening wetness appeared on his belly and the tip of his cock. He opened his eyes, meeting Shane's.

Damn, the man was gorgeous. He took off his glasses and placed them on the nightstand. He didn't need them this close up and they'd only get in the way. Then he slowly peeled off his clothes as Gray watched his every motion. Self-consciousness was impossible when Gray licked his lips as he focused on Shane's actions. Once he was completely nude, he reached behind him and pulled the end of his braid forward. He knew Gray loved his hair. Freeing the rubber band, he unbraided it, letting it fall around his body.

Gray moaned, his hips shifting on the mattress again. "Oh, God, Shane. Please get up here and touch me."

How could he deny such a sweet plea? He couldn't. Shane crawled onto the bed, sitting back on his knees between Gray's outstretched legs. Looking his fill, he ran his hands down Gray's taut stomach and thighs, never touching the leaking prick.

Gray growled at him. "You're evil!"

"Shh…I'm doing this, not you. You are supposed to feel and let me enjoy the work."

"Then get to the doing. Touch me, damn it."

Shane tugged some of his hair forward, twining it around Gray's cock and letting it slide away again. "Like this?" His hair almost tickled as it hit his own body. He wondered what it felt like surrounding Gray's penis.

Gray moaned, his hips pushing up, humping the air a little. Shane repeated his action, this time wrapping his hair with his hand firmly around the hair. He pumped several times, then let go. He lifted his hair away and brushed it across Gray's testicles, teasing him with it.

Gray gasped, his arms and abs flexing as he tried to grab Shane. Shane scooted lower so that he was eye level with the red and tightly drawn balls. Moving his hair to the side, he kept it out of his face but draped it over Gray's thigh. He licked a line from the base of Gray's dick down to the bottom of his balls, then back up again.

His lover's legs tensed and another low gravelly moan filled the air. Shane smiled and closed his mouth over Gray's testicles, sucking lightly. They were so close to his body that Shane had no problem getting both in his mouth. He inhaled the musky scent of Gray's flesh as he rubbed his face lightly against the other man's thigh. His own dick was aching with need now, but no way was he going to stop.

He snaked his tongue below Gray's balls, grazing the puckered hole he found there.

Gray grunted with need and raised his hips up, giving Shane better access. "Oh, fuck!"

Shane continued to lick and prod the best he could with his tongue with Gray tied. He thought about releasing one of Gray's legs so he could rim him better, but he didn't want to stop long enough to do so. Licking at the rosy opening, he made sure to get it completely wet and slippery. When he was satisfied there was enough moisture, he slipped a finger inside.

Gray gasped and immediately started thrusting and simultaneously pushing down, trying to take more of Shane's finger. He was so lovely in his complete abandon that he had Shane's own prick throbbing eagerly against the bed.

Shane grabbed Gray's hips, sliding up at the same time. He used his other hand to guide Gray's dick into his mouth.

"Oh, God. Oh. More..." Gray panted heavily, his body squirming.

Shane gulped him all the way down, sucking, as he fucked Gray with his digit. He pushed in hard, searching for the prostate gland. When he found it, Gray yelled and pumped deep into his mouth, nearly choking him. But Shane didn't care; he wanted his Gray begging and insane with lust.

Shane's dick dripped precome. He pressed it into the bed, his hips bucking just a little. He worked Gray faster. Soft slurping sounds filled the bedroom.

Gray pulled against the bindings on his wrists, slipping his hands out of them, and grabbed Shane, pulling him up, dislodging Shane's finger. Shane mouth released Gray's cock with a loud pop. Gray's lips crashed over Shane's. The kiss was fierce, all teeth and lips and tongue. It would have hurt if Shane wasn't so aroused.

"Fuck me." Gray pleaded.

Shane grabbed the pocket knife off the nightstand where he'd laid it and moved to the end of the bed to cut Gray's legs free. No way was he taking the time to untie them, Gray was desperate and so was he. He needed Gray as much as Gray needed him.

As Shane cut the ropes one by one, Gray bent his knees, exposing himself completely. Shane stopped for just a minute to appreciate the view as he closed the knife and tossed it aside.

Apparently he took too long, because Gray sat up and clasped Shane's cock, squeezing. "Now, Chief. Please."

It was a heady feeling knowing that he'd reduced Gray to one-word sentences. His sheriff wasn't overanalyzing every little detail now. Shane thrust into his lover's touch, feeling his stomach clench and his balls tighten. He didn't want to come like this; he wanted to be inside Gray when he spewed. He removed Gray's hand from his cock and pushed the younger man back onto the bed.

"Here." Gray handed him the lube. He slicked up his fingers and Gray's hole, then pushed two fingers in.

Gray moaned and pushed toward him, grinding his ass down onto Shane's fingers.

Shane leaned forward, capturing Gray's sopping prick into his mouth and sucking as he slid yet a third finger into Gray's ass, and then a fourth. He leaned back and looked down at Gray impaled on four of his fingers. The sight was fucking hot!

He couldn't wait any longer. Pulling his fingers out, Shane pushed Gray's legs up further and lined his cock up with Gray's anus, then pushed in with one hard thrust. Sweat ran down his temples and his hair stuck to him, but he was beyond caring as he fucked Gray with all he had. The only thing that matter was Gray's pleasure and his own.

Gray gasped, his eyes widening as they stared up into Shane's. He reached and grabbed some of Shane's hair, peeling it from Shane's sweaty chest and wrapped it around his own cock. He started stroking, Shane's hair between his hand and dick. Within seconds, Gray's muscles clamped down on Shane's shaft and his body grew taut. His eyes closed then snapped open, intent on Shane's as he came. "Chief..."

The gaze was so full of love and lust that it pushed Shane right over the edge. He felt the tale-tell tightening and just like that he shot deep into Gray's body.

Once his brain started working again he pulled free from his lover. Tipping his head back, he took in some deep and needed breaths, absorbing the scent of sex -- the scent of the two of them together. Suddenly, a section of his hair touched his body; a big wet, clumpy spot hit his thigh. Startled, he looked down at the white mess in his hair and heard a chuckle. He glanced into Gray's laughing green eyes.

"Your glasses are next."

Chapter Eleven

"What kind of beer? Do we get to pick since we're bringing it?" Shane nudged him lightly on the hip with the edge of the shopping cart.

"Yeah. Grab some Coronas for me and we'll get some limes. Then get whatever you want. John, Ethan and McCabe will drink anything, and Jamie doesn't really drink, so anything you want is fine. Just get a lot of it." Gray waved his hand toward the refrigeration unit that held all the beer, only half paying attention to his lover. He continued to stare down the aisle, frowning at the older woman who kept craning her neck around and stared down the aisle after she pushed her buggy past them. It was Mrs. Murphy, the town librarian, if he wasn't mistaken.

People were acting odd, and Gray was certain it wasn't his imagination. He was also pretty sure it was Shane they were staring at. Shane didn't seem to notice, but Gray didn't like it. Sherry Ann or her dad must have been running their mouths some more.

Gray casually walked to the end of the aisle while Shane put the cases of beer in their cart. He peeked around the corner.

Mrs. Murphy's eyes widened comically behind her big, round, plastic-rimmed glasses when she saw him, then she hurried on her way. Her short fluffy gray hair flounced with every step. What was that nosy old bat up to? Trying to get details for gossip no doubt. Damn that Sherry Ann! What could that girl possibly think to gain? Surely she realized her actions weren't going to make Shane hers. Then again, maybe it was just pique because Shane turned her down so many times.

"Grayson?" The pitch of Shane's voice said that it wasn't the first time he'd called.

"Yes?" Gray turned back to Shane, who was holding up a case of Budweiser.

"Yeah, that's fine. Just get that and the Coronas, then let's grab some limes and a bunch of chips. We don't need anything else since Jamie's making homemade salsa."

They found the rest of the things they were taking to poker night and checked out. Gray noticed more people acting furtive, clearly trying to appear like they weren't looking, but he decided ignore them. People could think what they wanted for now. The truth would come out sooner than later.

His resolve not to let it trouble him lasted until he was in the passenger side of Shane's truck with his eyes closed and head leaned head. You'd think people would realize that Shane couldn't possibly be guilty of having sex with Sherry Ann, much less knock her up. Most of these people had known the man for going on over twenty years, after all.

Gray sighed. He loved being back home, he truly did, and he loved being able to help the people he grew up with, but sometimes the small-mindedness really ate at him.

A soft caress landed on Gray's cheek, making him open his eyes and turn his head. He hadn't even noticed that Shane hadn't started the truck yet.

Shane smiled and leaned forward , brushing a kiss across Gray's lips. "Thank you, but stop it."

"Stop what? What are you thanking me for?" Had he missed something?

"Thank you for worrying about me and my reputation and for chasing down Mrs. Murphy to give her the evil eye. But stop thinking about it. You knew this would happen." Shane touched his forehead to Gray's, rubbing it back and forth.

"So you did notice."

"I did. Like I said, it's to be expected. Just think, these same people who are looking down their noses at me now will be telling everyone who will listen that they knew it wasn't true when Sherry Ann spills the beans."

Grey nodded and pulled Shane closer, cupping his cheek, caressing him with his thumb. "I know, but it's frustrating."

"Yes, but I don't want it ruining your evening. You've always cared too much and I love that about you. It's part of what makes you such a great sheriff, too. Most lawmen are so cynical, but you've managed to not let it take you over."

"I try really hard not to be. I don't judge people, not until I have all the facts. You taught me that."

"No, love, that's just the kind of man you are. Folks can be taught one thing but do another. Life makes us who we are and colors our perceptions, but it's who you are inside that counts. And caring about others and being fair is exactly who *you* are." Shane gazed at him with loving expression for a few seconds, then pressed his lips to Gray's. His tongue flicked across Gray's, seeking entrance.

Gray opened on a moan, happily kissing back. He snaked his hands around Shane's back, hugging him tight. He loved the feel of Shane up against him, the heat, the strength. He was finally starting to get used to the man kissing him, being with him. He wasn't sure that the "this is too good to be true" feeling would ever leave him, but at least he was getting over the "oh, my God, this is Shane" reaction.

Unfortunately, just as he was settling into the embrace, Shane pulled back. "We need to go. If we don't, something tells me we won't make it to poker night."

He was reluctant to release Shane, but his lover was right. He also thought maybe he'd just seen Mrs. Murphy's car go by, but he might have been mistaken. "Okay, Chief. Let's go play poker, drink beer, hang with our friends and have fun." He waggled his eyebrows. "Then we'll go home and have even more fun."

Shane grinned and started the truck. "I'll hold you to that."

* * *

"I fold." McCabe pushed back from the table and glanced at John, who'd passed out on the couch an hour ago. "I think I'm going home, if I can wake John up, that is."

Shane looked over at the sleeping man, then back to McCabe. "Go on, Gray and I can drop him off on our way back."

Jamie looked up from his cards, shook his head and set them on the table. "I'm out, too. Don't worry about big bro. If he's not awake by the time Shane and Gray leave, I'll bring him home in the morning."

McCabe shrugged. "Sure?"

"Yup." Jamie stretched.

"All right, then. Later, y'all." McCabe petted Fred, Jamie's German Shepherd, who was lying by the table, and left, a chorus of goodbyes following him out the door.

Jamie scooted back from the table. "I'm going to get more beer from the kitchen. Who wants what?"

Shane gave a quick glance at Gray, trying to decide how much Gray had had. Shane hadn't drank that many himself, but if Gray was going to be the one driving, he wasn't getting another.

His partner must have read his mind. He winked at Shane, then turned to Jamie. "I'm done. But I'll take a water or some tea."

Jamie nodded and faced Shane. "You want another?"

Shane downed the last sip in his can and held it out. "Yeah, I'll take one more."

Gray took Shane's empty can and stood up. "I'll help. I'm out this hand, too." He gathered the empty bottles and cans from the poker table and headed into the kitchen. Shane couldn't help but follow that gorgeous ass with his gaze as Gray left. The man was like his own personal magnet. Just as soon as they got home --

Jamie grabbed Ethan's empty bottle. "Another one, cowboy?"

Ethan contemplated his cards. "Huh? Oh. Yeah. A Corona with salt and lime. Thanks, babe."

Jamie followed Gray out, leaving Shane and Ethan to play.

Shane inspected his cards one last time, then looked at Ethan. "Your bet."

"Call."

Shane flipped his cards over. *Two aces.*

Ethan turned his. *A flush.*

Shane pushed all the game chips in the middle of the table toward Ethan and gathered up the cards. "Can I ask you something?"

Ethan glanced up from stacking his chips. "Yeah, what's up?"

"How bad was it when everyone found out you were gay?"

Ethan shrugged. "Other than being shot? Not too terribly bad. To be honest, I've been pretty surprised at how many people don't seem to care. Now, granted there are a few that won't talk to me now, but most people seem to be the same. Why?"

Shane shrugged and shuffled the cards. "Wondering what it would do to Grayson's career if it got out." That thought had been on his mind ever since Gray said they should tell his parents.

Ethan contemplated him for a minute. "I don't know, Shane. It's a small county. I'd like to say it wouldn't matter, but I can't. Who knows what goes through people's heads. If it were just me, I'd have never made any kind of public declaration. I'd have just let it be and live my life they way I want and let people draw their own conclusions. Of course, loving Jamie really didn't give me that option, since everyone knew about him. It was a safe bet that everyone was going to know about me since we were living together." Ethan grinned. "Gray's up for re-election this year?"

"Yeah."

Ethan nodded. "My advice, for what it's worth: if you feel like you just have to make it public knowledge -- and I'm not knocking you if you do, because God knows, Jamie would be out there marching in parades if I'd let him -- try to keep it quiet until after the election. That way it gives people another four years to see it makes no difference in how he does his job."

Shane sighed. Ethan confirmed exactly what he'd been thinking. "He's already been sheriff for four years."

Ethan nodded. "And you and I both know several people will forget that. If it comes out after he's elected, that gives him four more years where people are actively watching him because they know he's gay. It might not make a difference next time, but for now…"

Shane knew that, too. Hell, he'd only asked Ethan because he wanted someone to confirm his feelings. Not to brush it under the rug like Gray might. As far as he was concerned, his personal life was his business and to hell with everyone else. He didn't mind hiding, but he'd never had to on account of the fact that he didn't really date. And when he did, it was always out of town. But he was afraid to the Hunters about his relationship with their son for fear of their reaction, but he was also afraid of what it might mean for Gray. He wanted to protect Gray the best he could --

"Oh, my God! Suck it!" Gray's shout blasted from the kitchen.

"No!" Jamie yelled back.

Gray groaned. "Suck the head before it gets all over the floor."

"No, I don't like the taste!" Jamie's protests got louder. "Stop pushing my head!"

Shane's eyes shot toward the kitchen, then to Ethan, who was staring in the direction of the ruckus, an eyebrow raised and a smirk on his lips. He pushed back from the table and dipped his head, silently bidding Shane follow him.

Shane got up. He knew it couldn't possibly be what it sounded like -- and apparently from Ethan's wide grin, the other man felt the same, but what in the hell could they possibly be --

Jamie and Gray were standing in the middle of the kitchen. A foaming bottle of beer was in one of Jamie's hands, a closed beer can in the other. Jamie was holding the bottle away from him, trying to avoid the froth running down the container and his hand.

Meanwhile, Gray had a glass of tea in one hand, the other one on the back of Jamie's neck, pushing him toward the frothing beer. "I guess I was wrong. Maybe you were supposed to put the salt in before the lime. The lime wedge sort of blocked the salt."

The beer began to spill on the floor, Gray and Jamie both quickly shuffling their feet out of the way.

Shane fought his laughter, but when Ethan roared beside him, he lost it.

Gray looked up and beamed, shrugging his shoulders. "Who knew it was going to foam up like that?"

Chapter Twelve

Gray lay in bed staring at the clock. *3:00 a.m.*

When he and Shane had gotten home from poker night, Shane had kissed his cheek, crawled right into bed, snuggled up against him and was snoring minutes later. Unfortunately, Gray couldn't doze off himself. His mind was working overtime. Something was on Shane's mind, no doubt about it, and he wanted to know what it was.

After they'd left The Tin Star, Shane had been unusually quiet. Not that he gave Gray the silent treatment or anything, but he seemed inordinately preoccupied. Shane could almost always be persuaded to make love before going to sleep, but he hadn't so much as given Gray the chance to initiate anything.

Had he done something to irritate Shane? He didn't think so. Shane was pretty good at telling him when he was upset at him. One thing about his Chief was that he was a direct man for the most part. Plus, his actions prior to bed didn't indicate anger. But what was it? He didn't like to see Shane troubled.

An arm circled him from behind, pulling him out of his thoughts. Shane spooned lean hard body against him. Gray smiled and wiggled his back into Shane's front.

"Umm..." Shane's breath tickled his ear.

"Umm is right. You awake?"

"Sort of."

"Ahh..."

Shane's head lifted, peering hazily at him. "What's up?"

Gray rolled onto his back, so he could see Shane. "Can't sleep."

Shane managed to arch an eyebrow, but he still looked really drowsy. "Why not? What's going on?"

He chuckled. One thing he'd say for Shane, the man knew him well. Of course, the reverse was also true. They'd spent a lot of years together when they'd been younger. "You seemed preoccupied tonight. Something bothering you?"

Shane let out a breath and closed his eyes. Gray thought he'd gone back to sleep when he opened his eyes, looking a little more alert. "Just a little worried about what your coming out might mean to your career. It's why I've had you hold off telling your parents. Well, partly. I love them and don't want them thinking I took advantage of you."

Gray kissed him. It wasn't a passionate kiss but a gentle, "I'm here for you" touch of their lips. "You know my parents won't think that. They love you, too, just like you're one of theirs. As for my career..." He shrugged. "It doesn't matter, Chief. I'm not ashamed of you, and I don't want to hide you. You're part of my life."

Shane shut his eyes again, resting his forehead on Gray's shoulder. He stayed there for several seconds, then he kissed Gray's skin and pulled back. "The fact that your parents look at me like a son is part of my worry. I've known you most of your life, and I'm glad you aren't ashamed of me, but I don't want to be the reason you lose the job you enjoy or the love and respect of your parents."

"You worry too much, Chief."

Shane blinked, a smile spreading across his face. "That's kind of like the pot calling the kettle black, isn't it?"

Gray grinned, lifting one shoulder. "You're wrong: I don't worry; I identify the problem, analyze it, then come up with a solution."

Shane raised a brow, his grin still in place.

Gray chuckled. "Okay, fine. I worry. Sometimes."

Shane's smile faded and he became somber. "I'd still feel better if we kept it a secret a while longer."

"If that's what you want, Chief; just know it's not necessary. I won't advertise it, but I don't care who knows."

"Yeah, that's what I want, Grayson. Let's just get you re-elected this time and we'll deal with it after." He covered Gray's mouth with his own, his tongue slowly tracing Gray's lips, then pushing inside.

"Okay." Gray twined his arms around Shane's neck and pulled him down on top of him. He felt much better now. Maybe if he could get rid of his hard on, he could finally go to sleep. He pulled back and snaked a hand down between their bodies. "You going to fuck me now, old man?"

His answer was a nip on the chin and a muffled, "I'll show you old."

Shane slid off to lie next to him. His hand went under the covers and wrapped around Gray's erection. In no time at all, Shane had him harder than a rock and angling up into his hand, begging for relief.

Gray moved onto his side, reached down and wrapped his hand around Shane's cock. It jerked in his hand and the head was already damp with precome.

Shane moaned and thrust, still pumping Gray's dick. "Oh, yeah, just like that Grayson." He rested his head on his arm and stared into Gray's eyes.

Gray leaned forward, capturing Shane's lips and fucking his mouth with his tongue while he continued to jerk him off.

Their movements became frantic, their hands and hips all moving swiftly. Gray pushed moan after moan into Shane's mouth and Shane reciprocated. Their motions became sloppy and jerky.

Shane grunted and stopped kissing him, his mouth hanging open against Gray's. Spunk soon sprayed over Gray's hand.

Gray peaked too, his balls pulling up as they emptied into Shane's palm and the sheets.

After a few minutes Gray brought his own hand to his mouth, licking it clean. He loved the way Shane tasted, salty and slightly tangy.

Shane groaned, low and deep. "Damn it, that's unbelievably sexy!"

"Yeah?"

"Yeah."

"Mmm, well how about this? Is this sexy, too?" Gray slid under the covers and pulled Shane's half hard prick into his mouth.

"Shit!"

He licked Shane clean, lapped and suckled until Shane's dick went completely soft. Then he sucked the come off Shane's fingers as well before he glided back up the bed.

Shane tugged him forward into the wet spot, and kissed him. "You taste like us."

Gray smiled against his mouth, scooted backward and yanked Shane into the damp area. "Is that a good thing?"

"Definitely a good thing. It was really hot, but you get the wet spot for calling me old." Shane moved closer, then pulled Gray back into the middle of the bed.

* * *

"Son, can I see you in my office, please?"

Gray looked up from setting the table to find his father standing in the doorway of the dining room. "Sure, Dad." He set the last fork on the table.

Ted turned around and walked back out without another word.

Hookay... What was that about? He frowned. His dad hadn't seemed mad, but from his abrupt manner, it was evident that something wasn't right.

Shane came whistling into the room, carrying several glasses of tea, which he placed on the table. When he saw Gray, he stopped whistling. "What's wrong?"

"I don't know that anything is wrong. Dad just came and asked me to come to his office."

Shane arched a brow and stepped closer to Gray. His shoulders slumping a little. "You think he --"

Gray quickly gave him a one-armed hug and grinned. "I don't think nothing, Chief. He wasn't pissed off, if that's what you're afraid of, so relax. Go finish helping Mom get ready for dinner and I'll let you know what he says when I get back."

Shane nodded, his face still concerned. Gray traced Shane cheek with the back of his knuckles, trying to relax him, then he leaned in and kissed him.

Shane's eyes opened wide and he literally jumped away, looking rapidly around the room quickly before frowning at Gray. Gray chuckled and left.

He walked down the hall to his dad's office where he found the door open and his dad sitting at his desk, relaxed in his chair. Gray felt a little of his anxiety slip away.

"Shut the door, son."

Gray did so and went to lean on the back of one of the two leather chairs that sat in front of his dad's big oak desk. "What's up, Dad?"

"It's about the Broken H. About my and your mother's will."

Gray resisted the urge to groan. While he could see why it would be important to his parents after the close call his dad had had with his dad, he didn't want to think about either of his parents dying. Of course, he had his own will in order and had made doubly certain after he'd shot in the line of duty. Everything he had would go to Shane and his parents.

Gray stepped around the chair he was leaning on and took a seat. "Dad, do we have to do this? I don't want anything. Whatever you want me to have is fine. I'd much rather have you and Mom than any property or furniture or jewelry or whatever."

"I'm glad to hear that, Gray, and I'm not planning on keeling over anytime soon. But your mother and I have wanted to do this a long time ago. And it seems like now is the right time to do it. Ted folded his arms over his stomach and smiled. From the blue, he asked, "Are you and Shane involved?" It was almost a statement rather than a question, and he didn't sound angry or even surprised.

Gray, on the other hand, was stunned. How had they gone from a last will and testament to him and Shane? He knew his parents were sharp but, dang, that was incredibly perceptive of them. He really did think he'd have a little more time to get Shane used to the idea of his folks knowing about them. He cleared his throat. "Yes, sir."

Ted smiled, nodding slowly. "Well, I can't say that your mother -- or I, for that matter -- is happy about not having grandkids, but this does make things easy."

"I'm not following you, Dad. You aren't upset, which is kind of amazing, but in a good way. I really didn't expect you to be angry, but aren't you at least surprised?"

Geez! As soon as the words popped from his mouth, Gray could have slapped himself. There he went overanalyzing things again! Who cared if his dad wasn't shocked that he was gay or that he was a couple with Shane? He should be happy! He had the feeling that if Shane were here with him, he might have smacked him upside the head for looking a gift horse in the mouth.

Ted chuckled. "I've known, or maybe I should say I suspected, you were gay when you were a teenager, even while you were going from girlfriend to girlfriend."

"Are you saying you knew before I, er, admitted it to myself?"

"Yes, son. I may be a lot of things, but no one could ever accuse me of not knowing my boys."

Boys? Gray raised a brow. He knew his parents thought of Shane as a son, but was his dad saying he'd thought Gray and Shane had something going back even back then? That would upset Shane. "Dad, we weren't involved. We just --"

Ted held up a hand. "I know, I know. I just meant I've known for a long time that both you and Shane were gay. That's all. Stop scrutinizing things into the ground, Grayson."

Okay, okay, that's good. "How did you know?" *Like it matters?* Gray gave himself another mental slap.

"Son, does it really matter? You just can't help yourself, can you, boy?" His dad chuckled. "I knew because I'd have to have been both blind and an idiot to not notice how you used to watch Shane...and the way he used to look at you."

Gray had no argument for that. He could imagine what his dad had read in his face all those years ago. "But I dated girls..."

"Sure, one after another and none of them ever meant anything to you, only Shane caught your attention." Ted raised a brow. "I also know why you left home."

"You do?"

"Well, not the exact details, but I can guess. I'm assuming you made a pass at Shane and he turned you down, or something along those lines. It was bound to happen the way you followed him around. It didn't take a genius to see it coming."

Gray's mouth dropped open. Damn, had he really been that transparent? He squirmed in his seat.

"I can't say I'm happy that you left, but in a way I suppose it was inevitable. Shane may not be my blood, but I know that boy every bit as well as I do you. He would have turned you down if for no other reason than you're my son."

"Dad, I've followed Shane around and hung on his every word since I was a toddler."

"Yeah, but things changed when you turned, oh, about fourteen or so, didn't they? It was different."

Holy shit! Gray sat there dumbfounded. "If you knew why I wanted to leave, why didn't you say something?"

"How could I have stopped you? You needed to go, but I knew you'd be back. I hoped that when you did, you and Shane..."

"Huh?" Knowing his dad knew about him and Shane was one thing. Realizing that he actually wanted them together was another. "Dad, that's unreal! No one wants their kid to be gay."

"You're right, son, they don't. But it doesn't make them love their children less or not want the best for them."

"But that's just it, Dad, it does. Jamie Killian's dad --"

"Was an asshole who never loved his son in the first place." Ted shook his head sadly.

"All right, that was worse-case scenario, Dad, but still…a lot of parents disown their kids."

"Not a parent that truly loves their child. My point is, it's not the life I would have chosen for you…well, no, that's not what I want to say." Ted's forehead wrinkled in thought. "I'm very proud of you, son. What I mean is, I would have like for you to have married and have kids in addition to what you've already accomplished if for no other reason than it would have been easier on you, a lot less headaches. There are always going to be people who have a problem with you because of who you choose to love. It's not right, but it's life. But I can promise you this, your mother and I will never be one of those people. We just want you to be happy. And Shane, we want him happy, too, so if you two are happier together, well then…"

Son of a bitch! Don't that just beat all? Gray's eyes started watering. He blinked back the tears and smiled at his dad. "I love you, Pop."

His dad smiled back, his own eyes brimming. He dabbed his eyes with the back of his hand. "Okay, now that that's out of the way. I have some other things I want to talk about."

Gray chuckled and wiped at his own eyes. "That's not what you called me in here for?"

"Nope. I wanted to know if you had a problem with me dividing the ranch up between you and Shane if something should happen to me and your mother."

Gray thought about it. It was just a place, no matter how much he loved it, and it couldn't replace his parents. He knew he should probably feel a little slighted, but he didn't. It was only fair that Shane should have half the ranch. Hell, to be honest... "Dad, I don't deserve half. I haven't been here to take care of things. Shane is the one that has put his sweat, blood and tears into the place."

Ted waved the words away. "Nonsense! You are my son, and while you might not have been here, you would have come and helped if we'd needed you."

"Yes, I would have."

"Good, then that's settled. You don't have a problem sharing with Shane?"

"Not a chance! The Broken H, you and Mom are as much Shane's as you are mine." And Gray truly believed that. Even if something inconceivable should happen and he and Shane split up, Shane would always be a part of their family. He had as much right to the ranch as Gray did.

"Okay, now the bad news. I don't want you to tell Shane. He'll just argue and insist that I put everything in your name."

Gray started laughing so hard he couldn't catch his breath. It was true! Shane would have a fit when he found out. Once he finally stopped chortling, he nodded. "Okay, I'll keep it under wraps for now but, Dad, I can't not tell him forever. You really should let him know."

Ted chuckled and shook his head. "Oh, no! I'm not going to tell him; he's likely to belt me one for supposedly short-changing you. That boy always was overprotective where you're concerned. You break the news; I know he won't slug you. My part is done; now it's your turn."

Gray grinned broadly and settled back into his chair. If there was ever proof that Shane loved him, that was it -- that he always did what he felt was best for Gray. It had been and still was annoying at times, but the man's heart was in the right place. "That much is the honest to God truth. And for that very reason, I'm going to ask a favor of you."

"What's that, son? This sounds serious."

"Well, it's not so much for me as it is for Shane. Shane doesn't want everyone to know we're lovers. He's afraid it will hurt my chances at being sheriff again."

"You know he's right, don't you? It may very well mean you not getting re-elected."

"I do know, and to be perfectly honest, I don't care. I love what I do but I'm not embarrassed about who I am, and I'm damned sure not ashamed of Shane. However, I will need time to convince Shane he's more important to me than whether I'm re-elected or not." He shrugged. "Shane thinks we should keep it quiet until after this election and deal with it later. So, I'm going to try to do that...for him."

Ted smiled, got up from his chair and walked around his desk. "I love you, Grayson, and I'm very proud of you. You're a hell of a man."

Gray blinked away more tears, then stood up and pulled his old man into a big hug. "Same here, Dad!"

Ted patted his back, sniffled a bit, then pulled away. He rubbed his eyes and grinned at Gray. "Come on, dinner is almost ready and I've got to go tease the hell out of Shane about corrupting my baby boy."

Gray chuckled. "Okay, just make sure you tell him you aren't going to go screaming it from the rooftops yet."

"No, not yet...Not until after we get you re-elected. Then I'm telling everyone!"

Gray laughed. He truly had the best parents in the world.

Chapter Thirteen

"I can't believe after what you've done that you have the nerve to show your face around town, Cortez."

Shane didn't bother looking up from the freezer. He knew the voice and he refused to get into it with the man. He'd come to town to pick up a few groceries for Kaitlyn and himself, and that was what he was going to do. He grabbed a couple of TV dinners, put them in his buggy and walked away. With any luck, Kauffman would get the picture and just leave him be.

Kauffman shoved his right shoulder. "I'm talking to you, Cortez!"

Or not. He supposed he should have known better. Shane sighed and turned around. "Kauffman, I don't have anything to say to you. Why don't you let me get my shopping done, and I'll kindly take my face out of public." Shane about-faced and began pushing his cart again.

Kauffman growled and shoved him again, this time in the middle of his back.

Shane stopped and turned once more. He was not going to get into a fight with this man when whole ordeal was Kauffman's fault. If he had paid more attention to his daughter, she might not feel the need to lie outrageously to get attention. But Shane would be damned if he added fuel to the fire. "Do you even know if Sherry Ann is pregnant? Have you checked that out yet?"

"Are you calling my daughter a liar again?"

Shane shrugged. Hell, yes, he was. "Well, she's lying about me having had any sort of a relationship with her, so --"

With an angry growl, Kauffman hauled his fist back and aimed for Shane's face.

Shane stepped out of reach. His attention was focused solely on Kauffman as the man prepared to charge him, so he completely missed McCabe coming up behind Kauffman and catching him around the waist, stopping him in his tracks.

"Whoa, there! I don't think you want to do that." McCabe ducked as Kauffman spun and tried to land a blow on him as well.

Kauffman snarled and swung at McCabe for several seconds, before he realized he wasn't going to score a hit. "Fuck you, McCabe! This is none of your affair!" He pivoted, still fuming and turned on Shane again, jabbing a finger in Shane's direction. "You really have some nerve, you pathetic piece of shit! I heard the rumors Mrs. Murphy's been spreading. Rest assured that I'm not buying it. I know you're just trying give yourself an out. You want play the 'I'm gay' card, you go right ahead. I'm sure it will come in handy in persuading our sheriff into doing what's right!" Kauffman turned around and stalked off.

Ah, shit! Great, just what he needed.

"Well, I had it covered, but thanks, anyhow. Nice to know I still have a few friends. I'm guessing by all the talk flying around that friends might be hard to come by shortly."

McCabe grimaced. "Probably. Hate to say it, but that man isn't going to stop until he's run you through the mud and Gray right along with you. I'm surprised you haven't heard from that man's lawyer, yet."

"Hell, I'd welcome it! If he'll get the lawyers involved, my problem will be solved practically immediately. You know the first thing a lawyer's going do is have Sherry Ann go get a pregnancy test. Hell, Ted's already got our lawyer on it, but you know how long these damned things take."

McCabe shook his head. "Yeah, I hear you. Let me know if I can do anything to help. In the meanwhile, I'm going to go rescue my popsicles."

Shane chuckled without humor. "Later, man." He went back to shopping but couldn't pull his mind away from the feeling of impending doom. Yeah, he was probably being overly melodramatic, but this run in with Kauffman and the rumors already racing through town were not good things. The question was, how bad was it and how much worse would it get?

* * *

"Shane?" Gray stepped into the living room of his lover's cottage.

"In the kitchen."

Shane was putting together a sandwich of some sort. He turned from the counter and cocked his head at Gray. "What are you doing here?" He glanced at the clock on the oven, looking even more puzzled. "I thought you were staying home tonight?"

"Well, I hadn't heard from you all day, so I thought I'd stop by and check on you." He went to the fridge and pulled out a bottled water and leaned against the counter next to Shane.

"I was busy."

"You're always busy. How's today different?"

Shane looked him square in the eye. "What's on your mind, Grayson?"

Gray sighed. He didn't know what he'd thought to accomplish by tapdancing around the issue. He supposed he just wanted Shane to come out and tell him what happened at the store, but there was no hope for that now. He knew that look. Shane knew he was aware of what had happened. "Got a call from Ethan today."

Shane took a bite of his sandwich and shook his head. "Figures. In a town full of gossips, our friends are the worst ones."

"It's not gossip when it's fact." Gray frowned. "You weren't going to tell me?"

Shane chuckled. "Does it matter?"

"Hell, yes, it matters! I heard that Kauffman assaulted you! You should press charges. How's it going to look if you don't?"

Shane shook his head, stepped to the fridge and pulled out a cola. "He didn't assault me, and I'm not pressing charges."

Gray snorted. "If he so much as touched you, it's considered assault. I heard he pushed you more than once, Chief."

Shane popped the top on his beverage and took a swig. "I'm not filing charges, it'd just add fuel to the fire, so let's leave it at that. Your daddy has talked to his lawyers, so why don't we let them handle it."

Gray gritted his teeth. He couldn't force Shane to press charges, but damn it, Kauffman needed to be put in his place. He was already guilty of defamation of character by falsely accusing Shane of impregnating his daughter and verbal abuse. Now he'd gotten physical and Shane was just going to ignore it? Not if Gray could help it. "Shane."

Shane slammed his drink down on the countertop, the fluid sloshing out, and pointed his finger at Gray. "Don't...do not take that tone with me. I said no, now it's over!"

Gray thumped his own drink down on the counter, making water shoot out the top. "Need I remind you that part of this situation we find ourselves in is because you tried to ignore Sherry Ann's shenanigans in the first place. Do you have any idea what is going to happen when you fail to press charges? Folks are going to assume you did have an affair with Sherry Ann and now she's pregnant."

So much for holding his tongue. Gray knew better, but he couldn't stop himself. Shane's attitude had really set him on edge. It was the exact same one Shane had used to use to scold him when he was a child. He'd never yelled or even raised his voice much, but that tone brooked no argument. When Gray was younger it had always worked; he'd never have dreamed of arguing back. But now? Shane had better treat him like an equal!

and it was going to be open knowledge. Public officials generally didn't keep secrets for long. Someone, eventually, was going to be suspicious enough to uncover the truth. If not Kauffman, then someone else. Shane would be a fool to think he could protect Gray from that. Gray wasn't the type to broadcast his homosexuality, but he also wouldn't deny who he was.

Shane sat up and swung his feet over the edge of the bed. His skull throbbed. He felt like a horse had kicked him in the noggin. He rested his head in his hands for a few seconds, then heaved himself up off the bed and into the bathroom in search of some aspirin.

Shane looked in the mirror and groaned. He looked like he'd cried himself to sleep, his hair was all messed up, he had bags under his eyes and tear stains on his cheeks. Good grief, he was pitiful. He yanked the rubber band out of his hair -- ouch! -- untangled his hair and brushed it out. He rebraided it, cleaned his teeth, washed his face, and relieved himself before he surfaced from the bathroom. He glanced at the clock. *10:34 p.m.* If he left now, he could reach Gray's place in about half an hour. With any luck, Gray would be awake.

He was going to have to give Gray some credit. If there was one thing his Gray wasn't, it was an idiot. Gray had always thought things through before he jumped in. He had to have know that he might be outed at some point.

Shane retrieved his glasses from the nightstand and put them on. There must be something to the old saying about sleeping on problems, because he was thinking a whole lot clearer now. He'd been going about things the wrong way. Instead of wasting energy on hiding the fact that he and Gray were a couple, he should be trying to help the man get re-elected in spite of it.

No, he hadn't liked waking up without Gray one bit. He'd gotten used to Gray snuggled up against him every morning, whether were here or at Gray's place.

Shane stepped out of his room and into the hall. It was pretty dark. Hadn't he left the kitchen light on? The only illumination in the house was the moonlight peeking in from the windows. Shane moved into the quiet living room, his boot heels clicking on the tiled floor, then he stopped dead.

Gray was curled up in a blanket sound asleep on the couch. *He came back!*

Shane went to the couch, stepping over the bag at the end, and sat down beside Gray. It was light enough that he could make out the chiseled planes of Gray's face with just the beginnings of a five o'clock shadow. The man must be truly tired to the bone if he hadn't woken to the sound of Shane's boots or his movement on the sofa.

He leaned down and kissed the stubbly cheek.

Gray's eyes fluttered open. He grinned when his eyes found Shane. Shane thought he was absolutely irresistible. "Hey, Chief."

"Hello, love." Shane ran the back of his hand down the younger man's cheek. "I'm sorry, Grayson."

Gray nodded.

"I've got to stop trying to protect you. I have to trust that you know what's best for you. It's just hard to break myself of old habits. I've spent over half my life watching out for you, making sure things you didn't get hurt."

Gray pulled him down and kissed him. "Just stop trying to protect me from you. If there is one thing I don't need or want protecting from, it's you."

Shane caressed Gray's cheek, then stood. "I'll try; that's all I can promise. After all these years, it's kind of instinctual, you know."

Gray tugged him on top of him, hugging him and nuzzling his face into Shane's throat. "That's all I ask." Gray bit down where Shane's neck joined his shoulder. His cock was making its presence known under Shane's hip.

Oh, man, that wicked mouth was giving him goose bumps. At one especially erotic nip, he arched his neck, giving Gray better access and bumped the back of the couch. Shane shivered and slid his hands beneath the covers, finding Gray's naked chest. "Come to bed. I'm to old to make out on the sofa."

"Mmm. Okay, old man, lead the way." Gray gave his neck once last bite, squeezed his ass, then let go of him.

Shane groaned and got up, offering his hand. "I'll show you old man!"

"Hey, I'm just repeating what you said." Gray sat up, kicked his covers off and took Shane's hand. "Besides, I like it when you prove you aren't too old for certain things." He stood, his erect prick sticking out as if teasing, begging to be touched.

Shane sucked in a breath. Damn, the man was fine. Shane reached for Gray's cock the same time Gray went for his braid. Gray chuckled and proceeded to take the rubber band off and spread out his hair.

Shane squeezed and stroked lightly, eliciting a moan from his lover. God, he loved the feel of Grayson in his hand, hot and hard and smooth. He wrapped his free hand around the back of Gray's neck and pulled him closer. He loved that Gray was so close to him in height. It made things very convenient: his mouth was just right there, and his dick lined up perfectly.

He licked Gray's lower lip, then slid inside the moist cavern, his hand still gliding along Gray's shaft. Gray kissed him back, meeting his tongue stroke for stroke as the last of Shane's hair was freed from the braid. Gray sucked Shane's bottom lip into his mouth and began massaging his scalp. He pulled strands of Shane's hair forward, and let them fall. He drew back, his hands still tangled in the mass of black locks. "Love your hair, Chief. I want to feel it on my chest as you fuck me."

Shane groaned. If they didn't get to the bedroom now, they weren't going to make it. He released Gray's prick and grabbed his hand, tugging him down the hall into his room. As soon as they got there, Gray started on Shane's shirt. "Get naked, Chief. What are the fuck are you doing with all these clothes on, anyway?"

Shane chuckled and lifted his arms so Gray could yank the shirt off. "I was coming to get you."

"You had to get fully dressed to go to the living room?" Gray unhooked Shane's pants and worked his fingers into the waistband of the tight jeans and his underwear. He shoved them to Shane's hips, then went to his knees to work the garments the rest of the way down.

"I fell asleep in my clothes after you left. Aside from that, I thought you'd gone ho--" His breath caught.

Gray's mouth engulfed his prick even as his fingers continued to skillfully work Shane's clothes. Gray moaned around his penis, sending shivers down Shane's spine. Gray moved back. "Pick your foot up, Chief. I need to get your boots off."

Damned boots! Shane clutched Gray's shoulders and did as he was told.

Gray tugged off one boot, then the other. He looked gorgeous with his sleep-tousled hair in his eyes, intent on his task. Once he had removed Shane's socks, he discarded the jeans. Smiling up at Shane, a wicked gleam in his eye, he took Shane's cock into his mouth again. As he held Shane's gaze, he worked the prick in and out of his mouth slowly, deliciously.

Shane's balls drew up at the sight; a moan escaped him. It felt good, so good, but he didn't want to come like this. He needed Gray to orgasm with him. Caressing his lover's face, he stepped away, making his dick slip from Gray's mouth. "On the bed, Grayson."

Gray studied him, but thankfully didn't argue. He got on the bed and lay down, focused on Shane all the while. He spread his arms and legs wide.

Shane crawled up that luscious body, knowing how the feel of his mane tickling over Gray's legs drove him wild. He straddled Gray's thighs, then yanked off his glasses. He handed them to Gray.

Gray stretched to put them on the nightstand, then sighed and settled back, dropping his head onto the pillow.

Shane smiled and slid down to his lover's groin. He pushed Gray's legs further apart and shouldered his way between them.

Gray's head came off the pillow to watch him.

Shane blew a puff of warm breath over the lightly furred balls and licked one side, then the other.

"Oh, God, Chief." Gray grabbed for him. "Flip your legs around. Please."

Shane pulled one testicle into his mouth, sucking softly. He loved the feel of Gray in his mouth, the way he could make Gray beg for him, make him writhe with pleasure. It was amazing that this big, strong, tough lawman displayed such vulnerability to him. It was empowering.

"Please, Shane. Let me suck you, too."

Sounded like a good plan to him. He wanted to taste Gray, and Gray wanted him, so it was a win-win situation. Shane angled his body around.

Gray slid onto his side, bending his top knee and resting his foot on the bed, opening himself up. His stomach muscles rippled with the movement and his thick cock bobbed against his belly.

Shane admired the view for several seconds, mesmerized by his lover's body.

The sensation of hot breath was Shane's only warning before Gray took his cock down his throat in one fell swoop.

Shane bucked into Gray's mouth, his ass muscles clenching tight. He rested his cheek against the heated and throbbing prick in front of him for a moment. It felt divine. A smear of precome on his cheek let him know that Gray was also enjoying himself.

"Mmm..."

The vibration made Shane's spine tingle. He lifted his face and licked the head of Gray's cock, circling his tongue all around it before drawing it inside his mouth. He sucked lightly, tasting the tangy precome.

Gray's hips jerked just a bit, but he didn't stop mouthing Shane's prick. His head bobbed up and down, pulling Shane in deep, then sucking hard on the way out. God, the man could suck dick!

Shane tried to ignore the pleasure and concentrate on Gray, but his resolve lasted only seconds. Gray was too good at this and the sensation of Gray's prick in his own mouth had him in a near frenzy. He gripped Gray's hips and held them to take his cock in deep.

Gray moaned around his cock and returned the favor.

They worked each other hard and fast for several minutes, until Gray finally peaked, coating the back of Shane's throat with salty come. That was all it took to send Shane over the edge into bliss, too. He pumped his hips forward as he clung to Gray's ass, keeping his lover in place as he came.

Gray swallowed every last drop of his come.

Finally, they both lay in a boneless sprawl next to each other. He still had a hold of Gray's butt and Gray was nuzzling his face along Shane's hip. Shane kissed Gray's thigh and sat up.

Gray met him halfway, his hands going immediately to Shane's hair. They kissed long and slow, almost lazily. Shane lay back down, bringing Gray with him. His lover continued to play with his hair, twining it in his fingers.

Sometimes he'd wake up at night with Gray's face buried in his hair and his fingers tangled in it. Before Gray, he'd never slept with his hair down , but even when he went to bed with it braided, he'd awaken with it wound around Gray's hand or fingers. He smiled and kissed Grayson's nose. How could he have ever thought to give up man and what they had together?

"Are you sure this is what you want?"

Gray smiled back and covered his face with Shane's hair, inhaling deeply. He let it slip off his cheek, then focused on Shane's eyes. "I love my job, but I love you more."

Chapter Fifteen

Gray signaled, making a right onto his street. Thank God his day was over. He'd had a hell of a time concentrating on his work today, despite the great make-up sex. He'd certainly been mellow, but he needed sleep, too. Fortunately, he'd been at the office doing paperwork rather than out in the field. He wanted to go home to The Broken H. Funny how he'd started thinking of the ranch as home again.

He pulled into his drive and got out. There was something, a piece of paper it looked like, taped to the front door of the two bedroom, two bath, Craftsman bungalow he rented.

It turned out to be an envelope with his title and surname written on it. Gray used his key to unlock the door and grabbed the envelope on his way inside. No sooner had he opened his door than his cell phone rang. He shut and locked the door behind him before answering his phone. "Hunter."

"Are you still coming here for dinner, or do you want me to meet you somewhere?"

Gray smiled and ripped open the envelope. "Hey, Chief. I'll be there. I need to change clothes and grab a new uniform for tomorrow, then I'm on my way." Gray pulled out a typed letter, quickly glancing at the bottom where he saw his landlady's signature. That was odd, she usually just called him to tell him things.

"All right, then, I won't keep you. Your mom said to tell you she baked an apple pie today. You know, I like you coming to dinner. Kaitlyn is always baking things when you do. When it's just me and Ted, we get ice cream for dessert, not even homemade ice cream either. You're spoiled."

Gray chuckled. "If I'm spoiled, it's as much your fault as it is Mom's." He skimmed over the letter as he made his way to his bedroom.

Dear Sheriff Hunter,

I'm sorry to inform you that your lease will not be renewed. You have until next Friday to remove your things from this property.

Lois Wagner

"What the fuck?" That couldn't be right. Gray flipped the letter over. There was no explanation or anything else.

"Grayson, what's wrong?"

"My landlady isn't renewing my lease."

"Why?" Shane practically growled.

"I have no idea; there's reason given. Just a get your shit out by next week. Okay, I'm going to drop by her house on the way to the ranch. I'll let you know what's up when I get there."

"Can she do that? Isn't there a specific length of time she has to give you?"

"Yeah, written notice and a grace period, I believe. I'll have to check my lease to be sure. All right, I'm going to let you go. See you in about an hour, Chief."

"Drive carefully, Grayson."

Gray hung up and tossed his cell phone and the letter on to his bed. What was going on? He'd never been late with his rent, he obviously wasn't a troublemaker and he didn't throw loud parties. Maybe she had a buyer for the place? No, that couldn't be it, she'd have to have his permission to let people in to see the place. He shrugged and went to take a shower.

He was clean and dressed in no time, gathered his things for the following day and out the door within a half hour. He arrived at Mrs. Wagner's house to find two cars parked out front. *Damn!* She had company. Should he come back? It would be rude to just drop in if she had guests but then again her terse note had been discourteous, too.

Gray parked by the curb, strolled up to the front door and knocked. There was feminine laughter followed by the door being flung wide.

Mrs. Wagner appeared in the open doorway with a wide smile on her face, that faded as soon as she saw him. "Sheriff Hunter."

Gray looked past Mrs. Wagner and spotted Mrs. Murphy, the librarian and gossip hound, and Mrs. Kelly, the high school principal. They both stared at him, frowns on their faces. Mrs. Murphy actually shook her head at him. Well, guess that explained his land landlady's letter. Apparently she had a problem with him being gay. Gray gave Mrs. Murphy a icy look, then looked at Mrs. Wagner again.

He held the note up. "I guess Mrs. Murphy's presence explains this."

The woman at least had the good sense to realize that it was discrimination. She immediately started protesting. "Oh, no, that's not it at all. It's just --"

"That's quite all right, Mrs. Wagner. I find that I no longer want to associate with you, either. I'll have my things out by this weekend, I expect to have every penny of my deposit back." Gray spun around and left without another word.

The trip out to the ranch was only about a ten-minute drive, but Gray managed drag it out to twenty. He pulled up to the Broken H not nearly as excited about being there as he had been when he'd left work. Shane was going to flip over him being forced out of his rental. Oh, well, there was no hope for it. Better get it over with. He cut the engine and got out.

Shane was waiting for him on the back porch of the big house. He sat on the swing in a pair of khaki shorts and a blue T-shirt and white tennis shoes. His hair hung in a braid over his shoulder and trailed down his chest to his waist.

Gray smiled. When was the last time he saw Shane in shorts? The man sure had the legs for it -- long, leanly muscled and dark.

"What are you grinning at?"

"Just thinking you have nice legs." Gray stepped up on the porch and dropped down next to Shane.

Shane eyed Gray's bare legs and his denim shorts. "Your legs look pretty good, too, but you need a tan." He tried not to grin but failed miserably.

Gray scoffed. "I bet I've been out in the sun with my legs uncovered more than you have this year."

"Probably. I think you need to take me out in the sun. Maybe on the lake. We've got a boat, you know."

Gray grinned thinking about the twenty foot Bayliner his parents had bought a few years back. He'd never been on it. "Are you trying to tell me that I don't take you anywhere?"

Shane shrugged. "Just thought you might like to go waterskiing one weekend." He eyed Gray. "So, what was up with your land landlady? Why does she want you out?" Shane pushed off the porch with one foot, setting them to swinging.

Gray groaned. Apparently his reprieve was over. "Why do you think? Guess who was there when I went to talk to her?"

Shane's eyebrows pulled together. "Who?"

"Mrs. Busybody Murphy."

"She can't do that, Grayson. She can't not renew your lease because you're gay. That's discrimination and it's illegal."

Gray smiled humorlessly and ran his finger down the furrow on Shane's forehead, smoothing the lines. "I know that, Chief, but you and I also know that she can. Proving that's the reason she wants me to leave is next to impossible. She'd never admit to it. And I'm not going to spend money taking her to court to try and prove it when I'd rather not rent from a bigot anyway."

Shane frowned harder. "You don't sound too upset."

He shrugged. "I'm not. I knew it was a possibility. Besides, it's not like I spend a lot of time there. I'm better off to find something smaller and cheaper. And I'm always out here more often than not nowadays."

Shane put a hand on his nape and tugged. He kissed Gray's forehead. "You are amazing. I don't know how you can be so calm about this. It still pisses me off to no end when people act that way."

Gray nearly swallowed his tongue. He'd been expecting a rant on how this was Shane's fault, even though it certainly wasn't. "I knew a long time ago that this life wasn't going to be an easy row to hoe, but that's how it is, so I deal with it. As long as no one is targeting me because of who I love, which as we know isn't out of the realm of possibility, then I'm happy."

"You're absolutely right, of course, but I'm still amazed."

"Funny how people show their true colors when they find out you're gay, huh?"

"Yeah." Shane growled.

"Thank you."

"For what?"

"For not freaking out on me."

Shane got a strange look on his face, then it was gone, almost like it had never been there. He thumped Gray's shoulder. "I'm trying. It's not easy, but I'm working on squelching the urge to knock out your landlady." His eyes twinkled.

Gray chuckled and pushed him. "You nut!"

Shane laughed. "Seriously, I don't like it. But I'm trying to look on the bright side. You now need a new place, right?"

"Right."

"Move in with me."

Gray's eyes widened. "What?"

"You heard me; move into my house. Come live with me." Shane raised a brow.

He'd love to, he was here all the time anyway, but... "That would be like moving back in with my parents."

Shane snorted. "I am not your parent. You'd be moving in with your lover, your...partner, not your parents."

Partner, he liked that. "I know, but I'd be living off my folks. That isn't right."

"How do you figure?" Shane pointed at his small house. "That is my place. It came with the job. I pay for my own groceries and my electricity. You can pay half the groceries, electricity and upkeep."

Gray grabbed Shane, kissing him hard.

Shane grinned and returned his kisses. "Does that mean you'll move in with me?"

"Hell yeah!"

* * *

"Shane!"

Shane groaned at the summons. Who knew Gray would have so much shit? He set the last of Gray's clothes on his bed and went outside to see what Jamie -- or maybe it was

John, they sounded so much alike -- was yelling about. "What?"

Jamie had one end of an old, beat up, wooden desk; John had the other end. "Where do you want us to put this?" Jamie asked.

Shane glanced at the truck where Gray was handing boxes to Ethan and McCabe. "The wood pile?"

Gray looked up and frowned. "I like that desk."

"It's shit. How about we buy you a new one?" Shane looked the desk over again. It was an old roll-top that had seen better days. It appeared to be constructed of real wood, but over the years it had been painted, several times from the looks of it. The top coat was white but where the white was flaking off, it was red and there was a bit of green, too.

Gray growled menacingly at him. "It's an antique."

"More like a relic." Shane sighed. He'd agreed to give Gray the remaining bedroom for his office. The cottage's other two rooms were, of course, his own office and his, no, their, bedroom. "Okay, fine. But you're going to strip that thing and refinish it." He turned back Jamie and John, then jerked his head toward the front door and stepped out of the way. "Stick it in the last bedroom."

He let the two men pass and followed them inside, detouring to the kitchen. He grabbed six water bottles out of the fridge and took them out to the porch. Setting them down on the edge of the low wooden porch, he opened a bottle.

McCabe set a box, books it looked like, on the porch behind Shane and sat down beside him. He grabbed a bottle, held it up to Shane and dipped his head. "Thanks."

"You're welcome. Thanks for helping us move all this, er --"

"Crap?" Gray flopped down on Shane's other side with a chuckle and lay back on the porch. "Hand me a water, old man."

Shane poured a little of his own water onto Gray's belly.

"Ahh! Damn, that's cold!" Gray sat up and snatched the bottle from Shane, trying to douse him with it.

Shane grabbed his wrist just as Gray tipped the container. "You little shit!"

Gray smiled. "You started it." He relaxed his hold, then instantly shoved the bottle, upending it and soaking them both.

Shane sucked in a breath. "Ugh!" It was so hot from moving furniture that the cold water was a shock to the system.

Gray froze, his eyes wide, watching Shane, a smirk tugging at his lips.

Shane looked to his right, trying not to be obvious that he was checking out the other water bottles. When he glanced back, Gray's gaze was glued to the other bottles as well. Shane lunged for one as Gray practically dove over him, clutching his hand just as it wrapped around a bottle.

McCabe roared with laughter and smartly jumped out of the way, rescuing two of the other bottles before they got emptied.

Gray released his hand and scrambled for another bottle.

Shane unscrewed the lid on the one in his hand and dumped the contents down Gray's back.

"Ah! Shit!" Gray returned the favor and poured water over Shane's head.

Shane sputtered for a few seconds, then burst into laughter himself. He couldn't remember the last time he'd had so much fun. He and Gray used to do things like that all the time years ago when Gray was a kid. Shane had been in his early twenties at the time.

Gray leaned against him, arms resting on Shane's shoulders, his forehead against Shane's, laughing with him. When they finally stopped cackling like a couple of hyenas, they found the rest of their friends were gathered around the porch drinking their own water -- with the exception of Ethan, who was stealing drinks from Jamie's bottle.

Gray rose, shaking off water. "I'm going to go get more bottles. I'll get you one, too, Ethan."

Ethan shook his head, grabbed Jamie's water again and took another swig. "Nah, I'm good."

John, who was standing next to Jamie and Ethan, walked over to the porch and took a seat beside McCabe. "Is it safe now?"

Shane shrugged. "Depends."

John raise a brow, grinning from ear to ear. "On?"

"On whether or not Grayson decides to behave when he comes back." Shane looked over his shoulder just as Gray returned with two bottles.

Gray held up his hands, chuckling. "I'm behaving! Who wants one?"

Shane held out his hand. Gray raised a brow, tossed one to him and sat down on the other side of John.

Shane laughed. "Chicken!"

Gray put his thumbs under his arms, flapping them and making clucking noises. The others chuckled.

Shane shook his head and took a drink. The back screen door of the big house slammed, drawing everyone's attention. Kaitlyn was coming across the yard with a picnic basket and a tray that looked like it contained a pitcher of lemonade, some paper plates and cups. What a sweetheart she was.

Shane headed across the yard to help her. About a yard from the gravel drive between his house and the main ranch house, something hit him from the side. "Oof!"

It took him a few seconds to figure out Gray had tackled him. He was laughing before he hit the ground and so was Gray. Both of them went down in a tangle of arms and legs, rolling across the grass.

Kaitlyn laughed, too, and continued to his porch.

Gray finally got the upper hand by ending on top of Shane. He pinned Shane's hands beside his head and sat up, smiling down at him. He was still chortling and winded. "Hey, Chief."

"Hey, Grayson."

Gray finally caught most of his breath. He sat still for a few minutes, panting lightly, staring at Shane. "Thanks for letting me move in with you."

Shane felt good right down to his toes. He looked up into those happy green eyes and saw his future. He smiled. "Thanks for agreeing. It comes with a price though."

"Yeah?" One of Gray's eyebrows lifted "What price is that?"

"You can't ever move out again. You're stuck here, stuck with me."

Gray's eyes went serious, his grin faded and he dipped down and kissed Shane's lips. "That's a price I'm more than willing to pay." Gray got up and stretched out a hand.

Shane took Gray's help and stood facing him. "Good. I'm going to hold you to that." Then before Gray could evade him, he lowered his shoulder, planted it in Gray's stomach and lifted him into a fireman's carry, then took off toward the stables. "But you're still going in the water trough."

Chapter Sixteen

Gray clicked the mute button on the TV remote and sighed. It just didn't get any better than this. It seemed like he hadn't been able to get Shane to sit still long enough lately to just relax together. The man had been constantly on the go since Gray had moved in. He was either in his office, on the phone or out working on the ranch. It was almost like he was up to something, but Gray couldn't imagine what.

Gray lay his head back on Shane's shoulder. "This is nice."

Shane nuzzled his face against the side of Gray's. "This, watching TV, or this, snuggling up on the couch together?"

"All of this. Well, except for the fact that the commercials are so damn loud."

"Yes, they are. Tell me again why we're watching *Cops.* Don't you get tired of this at work?"

"Nah, I don't see this kind of action anymore. Our county is pretty small and there's also the city police. I mostly rescue kittens and stuff."

Shane laughed. "Rescue kittens? Isn't that the fireman's job?"

"Well, since we only have a volunteer fire department, nope. I get the rescue kitten calls."

"So, have you ever actually rescued a kitten from a tree?"

"Nah. But I did help Mavis Barnes get his goat out of the mud last summer."

Shane shook his head, bumping Gray's with his chin, a chuckle escaping. "I don't want to know. I can just imagine you and your deputies helping crazy old Mavis pull his goats out of the mud." Shane kissed his cheek and nuzzled against his neck. "Do you miss the action? Do you ever wish you were back in San Antone?"

Did he? Gray was quiet for several seconds while he thought about it, then he shook his head. "No. Not really. I liked the action, yes, but this is more rewarding. Here I get to help people I know, people I grew up with. I don't have to see the drug problems and gang crap like in the city. It's like being a small town sheriff, you know? I have some of the jurisdictional crap, the occasional domestic disturbance and the paper work and junk, but for the most part it's kind of like Andy Griffith's Mayberry. I like that."

Shane grinned against his neck. "Only you are a whole hell of a lot better looking that old Andy." He nipped Gray's ear. "Actually, I can see that. The county is mostly rural: farms and ranches. I'm sure you being an ex-rodeo star kind of helps, too. People respond to that kind of success."

Yes, they did. His rodeo wins had gone a long way to pave his way with the population. Some of it could be that he was local and his family owned one of the bigger ranches in the area, but the bull riding more than anything made him a local hero even though he'd never gone pro.

Gray turned his head. "You know what the one big bonus is about being here instead of San Antonio?"

"What?"

Gray rubbed Shane's thighs, kneading them. "You."

Shane tightened his arms around Gray's waist, pulling Gray's back flush up against his chest. He crossed his legs over Gray's thighs and leaned them both back on the couch again. "I'm no prize, Grayson, but I'm glad you think so." He nibbled on the back of Gray's neck.

Gray shifting his body slightly, studying Shane. "You are a prize to me, Chief.."

Shane brushed a hand through Gray's hair and kissed the side of his forehead. His eyes held Gray's for several quiet seconds, the look in them saying nothing and everything at the same time. Then Shane bit down on his neck.

"God!" Gray shivered. He couldn't decide if he loved the sensation of goose bumps or hated it. Then Shane's hand dropped from his waist to cup his cock.

"Geez, Chief."

Shane licked a long line up Gray's neck. He tilted Gray's chin and angled his face, then sealed their lips together.

Somehow or another Gray ended up lying on the couch with Shane on top of him. His lover continued to kiss his throat, moving down his chest as he divested Gray of his clothing. Shane didn't stop kissing and nibbling, worshiping Gray with his mouth, moaning as he slid down Gray's body. Once Shane had him bare from the waist up, he sat up and pulled his own shirt off. The muscles in his sleek chest flexed, making Gray's fingers itch to touch him. Gray reached for him, but Shane grabbed his hand and pulled it to his lips, kissing the back of it.

"No." He held Gray's gaze for a moment, then let go of his hand. He unbuttoned Gray's jeans and pulled them and his underwear off.

Gray's cock bobbed free, capturing Shane's undivided attention. "So, beautiful, Grayson." He settled between his legs. Shane stroked his prick a few times, then brought out his tongue, twirling it around and around Gray's navel.

Gray's stomach clenched tight. He reached for Gray's braid and started undoing it.

Shane handed his glasses to him, then went back to kissing and licking Gray's stomach.

"Have I mentioned how much I love these glasses?"

Shane smiled against his stomach. "No." He made it sound definite, leaving no room for doubt that he was answering a question Gray had yet to ask, rather than the one he'd just spoken.

Gray sighed and reached over his head, putting the glasses on the end table against the arm of the couch. "You're so mean to me."

Shane chuckled and nipped his hipbone. "I think you'll live." Clasping Gray's cock, he guided it to his mouth and took the head in, sucking lightly.

Okay, maybe Shane wasn't so mean after all. "Yeah, I think I'm going to make it."

Shane chuckled. "I thought so." He licked all the way down Gray's shaft to his balls before moving lower and settling his shoulders between Gray's thighs, spreading them wider. His tongue circled Gray's hole and pushed against it.

Gray's sucked in a deep breath. "Jesus, Shane!" His eyes closed on a moan, feeling boneless. The rimming was arousing, but it was also relaxing. He sighed and stretched out, getting more comfortable. He was in no hurry for Shane to stop.

"Mmm…" Shane's tongue continued to flick over his anus, circling and pushing. One of Shane's hand came up to tug on his balls; the other pushed his leg up and over, opening Gray wider. Shane was moaning softly against him with every lick. Abruptly, he sat up.

Gray's eyes shot open.

Shane rose and shucked his own pants, then he grabbed Gray's hand and started yanked. "Come on."

Gray groaned, but he stood up and followed his lover into their bedroom.

"We don't have lube in there." Shane pushed the bedroom door open.

"Note to self: stash lube in the living room."

Shane stopped when he reached the bed and turned toward Gray, sliding up against him. Their hard pricks nestled against each other. Shane's warm arms whipped around Gray's back. "Fine, but you explain it to your mother when she comes over to visit and finds it."

Gray shuddered. "That's just wrong, Shane. You can't mention my mother when I'm naked and hard and…yuck! That's just gross."

Shane pulled his bottom lip into his mouth, sucking on it. He grabbed Gray's ass in both his hands and rubbed their cocks together. "Doesn't feel like it's affected you any." He licked Gray's nipples. Hmm... Shane was awfully oral tonight. Not that Gray was complaining, of course.

He dropped his forehead onto Shane's shoulder and played with the long black hair there, rubbing it on his face. He loved the way Shane's mane always smelled like sunshine and vanilla. Threading his finger on each side of Shane's face, he pulled Shane's lips to his, kissed him, then finally pulled back and examined the deep brown eyes that gazed back at him. "Love you, Chief."

Shane stared at him for several seconds. Were his eyes tearing? He groaned and turned Gray until the backs of his legs were against the bed. "Lie down, love."

Gray eased back onto the bed and reached for Shane. He put his hands around Shane's lean hips and started pulling him forward, trying to get that gorgeous prick into his mouth, when Shane moved back.

"No. Not tonight." Shane walked around the bed to the nightstand, opened the drawer and pulled out the lube, setting it on the bed. Crawling up next to Gray. He straddled Gray's hips and leaned down to steal a kiss. His silky hair floated around him, brushing Gray's sides, his chest. Shane wrapped a length of hair around Gray's dick, pulling up, letting the dark strands rub against his shaft.

"Oh!" Gray bucked up into his hand. "Chief! Damn!"

Shane stroked him until Gray was writhing, pleading to come, then he abruptly stopped. He grabbed the lube and slicked his fingers up. Instead of putting them inside Gray, however, he leaned forward and slicked up his own anus.

Gray gasped. "What are you doing?" He was mesmerized. It was like a dream to have Shane leaning over him, lips a kiss away, his hair covering them both in a dark curtain. He'd never thought to top Shane. He didn't mind topping, but he preferred to bottom.

Shane's eyes closed in apparent bliss. "What does it look like I'm doing?"

"Why?" He would have never thought Shane would like being fucked. The man was so, so... Chief just wasn't the type to make himself vulnerable to others. And he would definitely see being topped as vulnerable. Gray blinked away the moisture in his eyes..

Those brown eyes blinked open, blurring before his own.

"I want you inside me."

"Why?"

Shane's lip twitched, then he grinned. "You sound like a broken record."

"Have you ever --"

Shane nodded. "Shh... Don't you ever get tired of analyzing the hell out of everything?" He reached forward and grabbed the lube again, squirting more onto his fingers. The whole time he got himself ready he stared into Gray's eyes.

Gray watched, his stomach in his throat. He couldn't decide whether to be nervous or excited; he was experiencing both. He had the feeling that Shane had never done this before. He knew Shane loved him, but the fact that he'd open himself to Gray and no one else was pretty heady stuff.

Shane's slick hand wrapped around Gray's prick and tugged twice, then he positioned the cock head against his anus. He pressed down and took him in, a little at a time. His expression was focused, intense.

Gray reached up and stroked his face. "Relax."

Shane took a deep breath and nodded -- then slid all the way down until his butt was resting against Gray's hips. His dark lashes fanned against his cheek as his body loosened up and accepted Gray.

"Shane." The sensation of heat and the way Shane's passage gripped him was indescribably wonderful. Gray grabbed a handful of hair and drew him forward. He held Shane tightly against him and kissed him fiercely, until they were both out of breath. He didn't want to let go, ever, and that was just fine because Shane didn't seem in any hurry to be let go either.

"You know what you mean to me, yeah?" Shane's mouth curved tenderly.

Gray nodded; he didn't trust his voice not to crack.

"Don't ever forget it. No matter what, okay?"

Again, Gray nodded.

Shane sat up and began to move, slowly at first, then faster, and faster still.

Gray was so incoherent with bliss, he was babbling. He squeezed his eyes shut, fisting the sheets in his hands. It was taking all his concentration to keep still. He wanted so badly to thrust, but he didn't dare. He would swear that Shane had never done this before, and he'd be damned if he hurt his Chief. He shook with the effort to remain motionless.

Shane untangled Gray's hand from the covers as he continued to ride Gray's cock. He placed it on his prick. "Touch me, Grayson."

Gray's balls drew tighter at the demand, and his stomach clenched. He stroked Shane's cock and tried not to orgasm, but it was useless. He shook his head, still working his lover's penis. "I...you...come!"

"That's it, love!" Shane stiffened above him, his dick pulsing in Gray's hand. Hot semen splashed against Gray's belly even as he spurted deep inside Shane's body.

After what seemed like an eternity, but was probably more like a few seconds, Shane collapsed on top of him, smearing the warm spunk on his stomach.

Gray gasped hoarsely, arms circling to Shane's back. Within minutes, Shane's soft breathing tickled his ear and he began to snore quietly. Gray lay there, surrounded by the mass of thick, dark hair and the welcome weight of his lover, in no hurry to move.

He didn't like the fact that Shane had been working so hard lately and that they hadn't seen much of each, but if this was how Shane made up for it... Nah, not even this was worth Shane exhausting himself. He brushed the mass of beautiful hair back and kissed the tanned forehead. "Night, Chief."

Chapter Seventeen

"Come on, boss!" Deputy Jameson jogged onto the sidewalk, grinning over his shoulder at Gray.

"Darren, where are we going?" Gray sighed. He still wasn't sure how Darren had convinced him to get coffee after work. It probably had to do with the way the kid refusing to take no for an answer. All Gray really wanted to do was go home to Shane, maybe watch some TV, then crash. He was exhausted. So exhausted, in fact, that he hadn't even realized Darren had actually entered the door *next* to the coffee shop instead of the cafe itself, until a bunch of voices yelled, "Surprise!"

Gray stepped back in shock. What in the --? There were red, white and blue streamers everywhere, and posters proclaiming "Hunter for Sheriff." It almost seemed like everyone he knew was there. His deputies, his parents, his friends, several community leaders. Gray looked around. Where was...

"Stop frowning; people are going to think you don't appreciate the effort they've gone to," a smooth voice drawled from behind him.

"Shane!" Gray turned.

His lover was standing right behind him, a huge grin on his face. Gray barely suppressed the urge to moan. Damn, the man was a walking wet dream. He'd dressed in a nice, red, button-down, short-sleeved shirt, a pair of blue jeans, black boots, his glasses -- best of all, his hair was down, hanging freely instead of its usual braid.

Gray couldn't help himself, he pulled Shane into a hug. Now all the phone calls and Shane's recent distraction made more sense. "You did this, didn't you?"

Shane returned his embrace and shrugged. "I had help. As good as you are and as much as we all adore you, you need some sort of a campaign to get re-elected."

"I would have gotten around to it."

"Well, now all you have to do is go around and kiss babies. We did the rest."

Gray threw his head back and laughed. People came up to him, talking about this and that. He ended up being swept away from Shane and into the endless questions, suggestions and comments from the crowd. There had to be close to a hundred people there. Shane, who was apparently now his new re-election manager, had thought of almost everything. From what he could tell all he had to do was get out there and be seen.

He drank some punch, ate a few cookies, talked politics, shared some jokes and shook several hands. He was even handed several large checks as campaign donations. It was incredibly heartwarming to see all this support and encouragement from folks who clearly wanted him to remain their sheriff for another four years.

After a couple of hours, Gray finally got a chance to catch his breath. He was relaxing at the refreshments table with Ethan and Jamie when he glanced up and noticed McCabe leaning against a wall, pretending not to watch John.

Jamie leaned in and whispered. "Weird, isn't it?"

Gray nodded. "Yeah. I can't figure it out. I would have sworn McCabe was straight."

"Me, too." Jamie frowned.

Hmm. He looked around the room.

"Over there." Ethan pointed. Gray's gaze followed Ethan's finger and caught sight of long black hair.

Shane was in a corner by himself, his back toward the room and his cell phone up to his ear.

"Am I that obvious?" Gray didn't take his attention from Shane's sinewy form.

Ethan chuckled. "Yeah." He slapped Gray on the back. "You've played nice and campaigned for over two hours. Go get your man."

Gray tossed his empty paper cup in the trash and made his way toward Shane, only stopping once to say hello to his parents. About halfway to across the room, Shane turned around.

Shane's jaw was set in a hard line, his eyebrows drawn together. "I don't know, Sarah. I'll have to call you back." He murmured in response to something said on the other end of the phone.

Gray blinked. *Sarah?* Shane's sister Sarah? Gray shook his head in wonder. Shane's family hadn't talked to him in twenty-six years and now one of them turned up from nowhere? What the fuck? Where were these people when Shane was sixteen?

Despite his career in law enforcement, Gray hadn't invaded Shane's obvious need for privacy to investigate his background, so he didn't know the exact circumstances of how Shane came to be at the Broken H; all he knew was that his dad had gone to town one morning and when he'd returned he'd brought Shane with him. He had once overheard his father telling someone that when he'd found Shane, the boy hadn't eaten in four days. Ted had hired Shane that same day and Shane had been at the ranch ever since. He'd even had a room in the big house until he became foreman and moved into the cottage, because Kaitlyn Hunter wasn't about to "let that boy shack up in the bunkhouse with all those old cowboys and no one to take care of him."

Maybe Gray was as protective as Shane after all, because he had the sudden violent urge to snatch Shane's cell phone, give his sister a piece of his mind, then hang up on her. All right, maybe he was overreacting. He didn't even know what Shane's sister, maybe his parents, too, wanted yet.

Shane rested his head on the headrest and let his lids cover his eyes. He was glad he'd ridden with the Hunters to the party, so now all he had to do was drive back with Gray. He'd worked very hard to get this campaign going for Gray, and the kick off seemed a big success so far. In the days of planning and talking to folks, he'd come to realize that perhaps Gray's sexuality would not be as big a deal as he'd first thought. People had actually come to him to volunteer to help in the re-election effort. And from what he could tell, most of those folks had already heard the rumors about him and Grayson. He was finally starting to believe that he probably hadn't ruined Gray's chances being sheriff again after all.

"Hey, Chief?" The truck turned a corner.

"Yeah?" He kept his eyes closed. Damn, he was tired.

"Who was on the phone?"

Shane blinked his eyes open and lifted his head. He glanced at Gray. "My sister."

"What did she want?"

"Me to go home. My father is dying. Seems he wants to see me."

"Are we going?"

"No." *Fuck them.* Shane looked out the window at the growing twilight. Suddenly, he felt every one of his forty-two years. Apparently, his parents had known where he was for years. They'd probably been contacted when Ted had enrolled him in school here and given permission for his academic and health records to be released. From what Sarah had said, their mom had told her how to get a hold of Shane. His sister had called the ranch and one of the hands had given her Shane's cell number.

Gray was quiet for several seconds as the truck turned another corner. "What if he wants to apologize, Shane?"

"Then that's his problem, not mine. If he was truly sorry he'd have never kicked me out in the first place."

"Hmm..." Gray seemed to think about it. "The man is dying. People make mistakes."

"A mistake is adding up numbers wrong or spilling coffee in your lap. Forcing your only son from his home because he's gay isn't a mistake. It's hateful and cruel and... I don't want to talk about it, Grayson." He did not want Gray to know all the sordid details. He'd told his sister that he wasn't going back to New Mexico and that he didn't want to hear from her or the rest of his family again. He had put them behind him where they belonged and had moved on long ago.

Shane pinched the bridge of his nose with a thumb and forefinger. His life was here, with Gray and with the Hunters. Ted and Kaitlyn were more parents to him than his flesh and blood had ever been. They loved him, and he loved them.

"Shane --"

"You have no fucking clue, Grayson, so stay out of it!" Shane winced. He hadn't meant to be so harsh, but he really didn't want to talk about it. He'd overcome that period in his life and he refused to look back. Certainly not now, when he didn't need yet another reminder that Grayson was too damned good for the likes of him.

Gray turned another corner, the last one on the way to the ranch. When he spoke his voice was soft, soothing. "I don't know what all happened to you, Chief, but I know you. I know that if you don't go, you'll beat yourself up over it later. If nothing else, just go to show them all what you've become without them. Go show them that you didn't need them and you made it by yourself just fine. Hell, go so you can tell the old bastard off one last time while he's still around to hear it."

Goddamnit, his head hurt! "I'm working on your campaign and too busy to go. I'm doing my damnedest to see that you every have opportunity to remain in office. In fact, I've been working my ass off to get you what you want."

Gray pulled up to the house and parked. He turned and laid his hand on Shane's shoulder. "I don't need you to get me what I want. You don't have to try and fill my every desire. Besides, I already have everything I could possibly want -- with the current exception of my partner's happiness."

"I'm happy!" Shane shrugged off Gray's hand and got out of the truck. He didn't need Gray fawning over him. It was his job to take care of things, not the other way around. The last thing he wanted to do was burden Grayson any more than he already did. He made it up to the porch steps and got the key in his door before Gray caught up to him.

"Yeah, you sound real damned happy." Shane swore he could hear Gray's teeth grinding together.

Shane shoved the door open. "If you will just shut up about my goddamned family, I will be happy."

Gray held his hands up.

Shane sighed. "Look, I'm sorry. I've been pretty busy and I'm exhausted. I want to give you the best campaign I can and my family has nothing to do with that or with us, all right?"

"I'd rather have you rested and happy than stay sheriff. I can do other things, you know. I can work here, for you, for instance. Or I can get a job on one of the smaller cop shops around here."

Shane nodded. He did know all that, but he still had to do what he could for Gray. He would have put his best effort in it anyway, but it seemed even more important now because he was the reason Gray might not get re-elected in the first place.

Gray pulled him close, kissing his temple. "Come on, Chief. Let's get you in the shower, then bed. You'll feel much better after that."

He let Gray lead him to their bathroom. "I'm the one that is supposed to take care of you."

Gray flipped on the bedroom light. "Who says so, Chief?"

"I do."

Gray went to the bathroom and turned on the water. "Did it ever occur to you that I might like to take care of you once in a while?"

"No."

Gray grinned and came back out and began undressing him. When he had Shane naked, he started on his own clothes. "Well, I do. You'll just have to suck it up like a man and let me." Gray got rid of the last of his clothes and shoved Shane toward the shower.

"I don't want to get my hair wet, it takes forever to dry."

Gray rummaged through the drawers on the vanity and came up with an elastic band. Gray, bless him, had bought a ton of the things and stashed them all over the place. Shane no longer broke the damned things, and now he always had one handy.

Gray parted Shane's hair and buried his face in it, inhaling strongly. "Thank you for wearing it down for me."

Shane grinned. "You noticed."

Gray hugged him fiercely, his face still buried in Shane's mane. "Of course, I did. You did leave it down for me, right?" He pushed his hips against Shane's butt; Shane could feel he was already hard. Gray took one last deep breath, parted Shane's hair and braided it.

Shane groaned, pushing his ass back against Gray's erection. His own cock had stiffened the instant Gray had begun undressing him. "Uh huh." Leave it to Gray to cheer him up, just like he always had. "Grayson?"

Gray wrapped the elastic band around the end of his braid and moved away. He tested the water and jerked his head to the side, indicating that Shane should get in. "What?"

"I want you."

"You've got me. Get in."

Shane stepped into the steamy stall and turned, waiting for Gray to join him. As soon as Gray closed the shower door, he moved into Shane's arms. Shane tugged him close, bringing their mouths together. He kissed Gray, then pulled back just a little. "Thank you."

"For what?"

Shane closed his eyes and rested his forehead on Gray's. "For being you, love."

Gray let out a little moan and pressed his lips to Shane's. His hand reached down and gripped Shane's cock, squeezing and stroking lightly.

Shane grunted into his mouth and tried to return the favor.

Gray shook his head, breaking their kiss. "Just feel."

"But --"

"Shh..." Gray slid to his knees -- and sucked him right in. He grabbed Shane's hips with both hands and drew him closer. He suctioned off Shane without mercy, setting up a fast pace and rhythm.

In mere seconds, Shane's hips were snapping to and fro, fucking Gray's greedy mouth. His fingers tangled in Gray's hair, knowing Gray loved it when he did that. He watched his cock disappear into that hot moist cavern over and over again, marveling at the erotic sight. Those greener-than-grass eyes peered up at him as Gray's nose abruptly buried into his pubes. Shane lost it. He came with deep moan, pouring himself endlessly down his lover's throat.

Gray held him between his lips until Shane was limp, then got up. Gray kissed him, then spun him around. "Let's get you cleaned and into bed." He voice was sexy, a little husky.

Shane tried to protest, and turn back toward Gray, but Gray wouldn't allow it.

"Let me take care of you. You haven't come yet."

Gray chuckled and started soaping him up. "You're out of it, aren't you, Chief? I came just before you did. Relax and let me do something for you for once." He kissed the nape of Shane's neck and murmured softly against his skin. "I love you, Shane."

Shane nodded, very near tears; it was all he could do. Damn, he was a mess, but it had all finally fallen into place. No matter what his parents had put him through, he couldn't regret it because he'd gotten Gray from their actions. For that alone, he couldn't hang on to his anger any longer.

Now he just had to work up the nerve to tell Gray the whole story about his past.

Chapter Eighteen

Shane closed the back door quietly behind him and carried his cup of coffee to the back porch rail. He hadn't been able to sleep and he didn't want to wake Gray, so he'd thrown on a pair of flannel sleep pants, put on his glasses and gone to make coffee. Ironically, Grayson was the one who usually lost sleep thinking, not him.

He lifted a leg and sat onto the wooden railing. His braid was in the way under him, so he flipped it over his shoulder to rest on his chest, then leaned back against the post. It wasn't the most comfortable spot, because his butt didn't quite fit on the rail, but it was better than sitting on the ground since Gray had taken all the lawn chairs to the front porch.

There was a soft breeze blowing. It felt really good on his bare feet and chest, creating just the right atmosphere and temperature. Texas was nothing if not hot in the summer, even at night, so the breeze was much appreciated.

Shane took a sip of coffee and looked out over the quiet south pasture. The Johnson grass swayed in the moonlight and crickets were chirping. It was beautiful out here at night; he could see the stars twinkling above in the endless black sky. *This* was his home, and it had been for the over twenty-five years. He wasn't going back to New Mexico. There was nothing there for him now. He didn't belong there and those people meant nothing to him anymore.

Taking another drink, he closed his eyes and rested his head on the post. His family had known how to find him, but in all the time he'd lived here, they hadn't once tried to contact him. Until now, that is. Now that they wanted something from him.

His father was dying, Sarah had said. The thing was, that man from his past wasn't his father. No. His father was sound asleep in the big white house that sat thirty feet away.

Funny how things in life tended to go full circle. He'd thought he was done with believing he wasn't good enough for Gray, but here he was again. The reminder of how he'd got here and what he'd gone through had him feeling inadequate again. He knew Gray though, and he was certain Grayson wouldn't stop loving him once he knew the whole story, but even still there was that little shadow of doubt. Thinking about his biological family always did that to him...made him doubt himself.

Shane took one last swallow from his cup, then tossed the rest of the contents into the grass. He set his cup behind him on the rail, eyes still closed, enjoying the feeling of the wind on his face. Maybe he was a cold-hearted bastard, he didn't know -- and he didn't care. He'd put the pain behind him…well mostly. After he told Gray, it would be done with and finally, irrevocably over.

Something snapped behind Shane, pulling him out of his thoughts and forcing his eyes open. There was a rustling, as if someone or something was moving around the side of the house. He sat really still, listening. There it was again, rustling like someone walking through the grass. Must be one of the hands taking a stroll, though they usually didn't come back here.

Only the fence to the south pasture lay near Shane's back porch. All the outbuildings, stables and barns and such, were to the left of his cottage. The bunkhouse was even further out past them. The structures over here in this area were his cottage and the big house, giving him and the Hunters a bit of privacy from the day-to-day operation of the ranch.

Shane turned his head and straightened up slowly. He didn't want to startle whichever one of his hands was out wandering around.

"Well, hell, Cortez, you're making this easy."

Shane started at the voice. His anger kicked in. What the fuck was that man doing on his property this time of night? He pivoted on the porch, swiveling to face the man as the trespasser came into sight.

Kauffman. Sherry Ann's dad strolled into the clearing between the fence and Shane's porch. He held a shotgun over steadily pointing at Shane.

Shane's stomach dropped to his feet. Great, just great. Figured, didn't it, that he'd worked out his family issues and had realized how blessed he was, but now he was probably going to die. Well, screw that! He had too much to live for.

He had to keep Kauffman from shooting him, otherwise Gray would hear the blast and come out to investigate. What if the man hurt Gray? He couldn't risk that. He couldn't risk his brave. "What are you doing here, Kauffman?"

"What the fuck do you think I'm doing here, Cortez? You think you can get away with using my daughter and treating her like trash?" Kauffman jabbed the shotgun forward, punctuating each word.

Shane held his hands up in the universal "I'm unarmed, don't hurt me" gesture. "Kauffman, I swear to you that haven't done anything to Sherry Ann."

"She's pregnant, damn you! The test came back positive." Kauffman moved closer, gun aimed at the middle of Shane's bare chest.

Shane glanced around using only his eyes, making certain to keep his head and body still. He searched for something, anything to get him out of this situation in one piece. He needed time. "It isn't mine." Shane side-stepped, putting the post in front of him. It wasn't much cover, but it was better than nothing.

"Sherry Ann says it is." The man shifted along with Shane.

"What will killing me solve? Why don't you put the gun down and we can talk about this." Something moved in Shane's peripheral vision by the end of the house. *Gray.*

He had to keep Kauffman's attention centered on him; he didn't dare think of what might happen if he didn't. He raised his voice a little, not a shout, but louder. "You know you'll land in jail. If Grayson doesn't come out of the house and kill you after you shoot me, you'll end up in prison. Think of what that will do to your daughter, your reputation, your business. You aren't going to do Sherry Ann any good if you're behind --"

"Daddy?" Sherry Ann came running around the same side of the cottage as her father had, the opposite direction from Gray.

Kauffman abruptly jerked his attention and his gun away from Shane.

Everything somehow slowed down. Shane's focus rested solely on the Kauffman as he leapt over the rail and rushed the man. Eyes trained on the shotgun, he was distantly aware of Sherry Ann's horrified gasp and Gray racing forward. In hindsight, it would probably seem a insanely stupid thing to do, but all he could think of then was that he had to get that weapon away from Kauffman.

Just as he was about on top of the man, Kauffman spotted him and tried to raise the shotgun again.

"Daddy! No!" Sherry Ann ran toward her father, arms spread out.

In an instant, time suddenly seemed to fast forward once more.

Shane grabbed the barrel of the gun and yanked it away.

"Don't fucking move, Kauffman!" Gray stood about five feet away. "Put your hands on your head!" He was barefoot and bare-chested, his jeans on but unfastened. His hair stuck straight up, but at the moment Shane couldn't conceive of a better vision.

Shane turned the shotgun around, aiming it at Kauffman as he backed out of immediate reach.

Sherry Ann had stopped halfway to her father.

Kauffman pivoted slowly toward Gray, putting his hands on his head as he did so.

Shane heaved a sigh of relief. "Sherry Ann, get over here out of the way."

She shook her head, sobbing. "No. No. This is all my fault."

Kauffman turned to glare at Shane but didn't make any other move. "No, honey, it's not. It's his fault."

"No, Daddy. Shane didn't do anything. I'm not pregnant. I tried to get him to go out with me, but he wouldn't. I'm sorry."

"What?!" Kauffman dropped his hands and spun toward his daughter.

"Hands back on your head, Kauffman!" Gray shouted, moving closer.

Kauffman put his hands back, his shoulders sagging in clear disbelief. "What? Why would you say such a thing? You're lying now, aren't you? You're trying to protect him! What about the pregnancy test results?"

Sherry Ann slumped to the ground and bawled. "I-I got a urine sample from my friend Kelly! I'm s-sorry!"

The older man turned back to Shane shaking his head, mouth working silently. The man looked defeated.

Shane felt like hell, even though it was the man's own fault. If he'd paid more attention to his daughter, showed her some affection, none of this shit would have happened. But at least he apparently loved his kid enough to kill for her. What that said for anything, Shane didn't know. And then, there were the consequences of his actions tonight; what was he going to get for demonstrating his love so late and in this way? Maybe --

"No, Chief. Absolutely not! Don't you even ask me. He's going to jail."

Shane nodded. Gray was right. It seemed the man's heart was in the right place after all, but he needed to learn to use his head. Shane glanced at Sherry Ann, still sobbing wildly on the ground. If nothing else, Kauffman going to jail would be a good lesson for her. Maybe, like her father was about to find out, she'd be better to think before she acted next time.

* * *

Gray shut the door after waving his parents off. When his deputies had shown up, all the ruckus had woken his parents. His folks had hugged, kissed and cried all over Shane, then turned around and done the same to him. He loved them both but, dang, he was glad when they finally went back to bed. His deputies had left an hour ago to take Sherry Ann to a friend's house and Kauffman to jail.

He needed Shane.

Resting his head on the door, he thought about what had happened. How he'd roused to find the bed empty and Kauffman yelling outside his window. Talk about coming fully awake and hitting the ground running. He let out a deep breath.

A hand landed on his shoulder, tugging him around. He swept his arms around Shane and buried his face in the crook of his lover's neck. He inhaled, letting Shane's unique spicy scent invade his senses. They stood there for the longest time, just holding each other.

After several minutes, Shane spoke. "Thanks, love."

"You're welcome." He leaned in for a kiss, but Shane stepped back. Gray frowned.

Shane smiled faintly and led Gray to the couch. "I need to tell you something." He sat and faced Gray, face serious, almost grim.

Gray tried to swallow the lump in his throat. "Is this something I'm not going to like?"

Shane dipped his head once, his jaw tight. "Probably. I want to tell you how I ended up here at the Broken H. Not even your parents know the whole story." He ran his hand down his face, a sure sign that he was nervous.

Gray reached for Shane to pull him close again, but Shane shook his head.

"Just let me tell you, then you can decide whether you still want me or not."

Gray blinked, completely dumbfounded. Shane was afraid that whatever he had to say was going to change the way Gray felt about him? That was never going to happen, but it was clear he wasn't going to be given the chance to try and convince Shane otherwise right now. That would likely take too long, and the sooner Shane said what he needed to say, the sooner he could hold him, assure himself that Shane was still here. Still safe and in one piece. He nodded. "Go ahead."

"Both my parents are full-blooded Apache. They are or were both active in the tribal council, but we didn't live on the reservation. My father was a college professor and my mother taught high school math."

It made sense, since Shane had a really high IQ. It was probably due in part to his parents pestering him to study and shoving information at him, Gray thought, barely stifling his movement toward his lover again.

"I'm the oldest and Sarah is two years younger than me. We were pretty much the typical middle-class family, but with Apache customs. Everything was great until I turned fifteen and really admitted to myself that I was gay. I had known before then, but I'd tried my best to be normal -- or what I'd always been taught was normal. I managed to get part of it right." Shane snorted. "I was at the head of my class academically and the second string quarterback. I was even one of two freshmen that made the A team and in several tribal youth organizations. You could say I was considered the perfect son, until my parents caught me one evening making out on the couch with another guy."

"And they kicked you out." Gray had known it was coming, but it still hurt him.

Shane smiled without humor and shook his head. "Oh, no! That would probably have been easier to deal with. They didn't kick me out at all; in fact, they didn't do anything. The Apache cherish their children, you see, so they wouldn't have felt right about making me leave. What would their friends and family have said?

"No, they just ignored me -- when they weren't telling me how worthless I was or what a big disappointment I had turned out to be." Shane stared off into space. The look on his face was haunted. "I went from being the golden boy to the elephant in the room. They didn't come to my football games, they no longer cared about my grades. They only spoke to me if I was in their way and they wanted me to move. They quite literally froze me out of their lives and my home." He looked at Gray, his eyes once again focused, and shrugged. "I couldn't bear to be there any longer, so I left."

Fuck! Talk about cruel and undeserving punishment. "I thought Native American cultures were more open when it came to homosexuality."

Shane shrugged again. "Some are. They call us two spirits or Berdache. But not the Apache or, more specifically, not our particular tribe." Shane laughed, the sound rusty and painful to hear. "Heck, my parents didn't even admit that I was gay. Who knows what they eventually told people." His lip trembled slightly.

Seeing that nearly broke Gray's heart; he held out his arms. He needed to soothe himself as much as Shane.

Shane shook his head. "Wait, there's more." Shane closed his eyes and took a deep breath. "I filled a duffle with clothes and some food from our pantry and started walking. I had no idea where I was going; I just had to leave. I didn't wander far at first. I stayed in the area hoping they'd come for me. I thought that they'd at least report me missing. After a couple of days, when it was obvious that they didn't want me back, I started hitching.

Shane's voice cracked a little. "I ended up in Amarillo before I started giving blowjobs for rides and food. I'm not proud of how I managed to get here, but it was all I had at the time. The last ride, the one that got me here, I refused to give more than a blowjob. I was so tired and weak from hunger that the guy managed to open the door and push me out while the car was still moving. I landed in oncoming traffic and your dad almost ran over me." Tears streaked from his lids and ran down his cheeks, plopping on to his pajama bottoms. "That's how I met him. Ted stopped and helped me into his truck. He tried to take me to the hospital, but I wouldn't go. So he fed me at Betty's diner." He smiled briefly. "Ted managed to drag it out of me that I was homeless, so he offered me a job and brought me home to Kaitlyn... Well, you know the rest."

Gray closed his own eyes, attempted to keep the moisture from falling, but it was no use. The tears came anyway. What if he'd been born to parents like Shane's? Thank God for his parents! He was an incredibly lucky man, and he owed them both more than he could ever pay -- for himself and for Shane.

He sat there for a few minutes, trying to form words, but they wouldn't come. Finally, he gave up and grabbed Shane, embracing him.

Shane attempted to move away for half an instant, then he wrapped his arms and legs around Gray, putting his head on Gray's chest.

Gray swallowed the lump in his throat and his tears, and rubbed Shane's back. He could feel moisture sliding off his chest and down his belly, then Shane's shoulders started to shake. Gray kissed the back of his neck and continued to stroke. His own tears rolled down Shane's shoulder, but he just held Shane even tighter. As an officer in San Antonio, he'd seen and heard shit like this all the time, but somehow knowing it was his Chief who had experienced it, who had suffered, really drove the point home. He decided then and there that Shane's parents didn't deserve Shane and it no longer mattered what they wanted. He wouldn't force Shane to return to New Mexico.

Shane took a shaky breath and clutched at him. "The worst part of everything was that I really expected them to try and find me. When they didn't, I felt as worthless as they told me I was."

"You're not worthless!"

"I know. You know when I finally realized it?"

Gray pulled back, looking into red, watery, brown eyes. "When?"

Shane smiled and touched his cheek. "The day after I got here when I met you. You looked up at me with these big green eyes full of awe and you asked me --"

Gray smiled back, his tears coming faster now. Shane's face blurred in his vision but he finished the sentence. "Are you a war chief or a peace chief?"

Shane brushed a tear off Gray's face with his thumb and sniffed, visibly getting himself together. "You looked up at me with such wonder in your eyes, such respect, that I realized I couldn't possibly be useless. From that day on, I knew I was somebody who meant something, who had a place in the world, because you admired me."

"I still do. There aren't many men who deserve as much respect as you do."

Shane trembled. "I was half afraid that after you knew the truth you would be ashamed."

Gray tilted his upward to stem the flow of tears and shook his head. God, what a pair they made. Crying and clinging to each other like a couple of girls when they'd already faced down a guy with a shotgun cool as you please. He almost laughed. "Knowing how you got here and what you went through only makes me love you more. And you know what?"

"What?"

"I finally have an answer to that question."

Shane frowned. "What question?"

"What kind of chief you are."

Shane smiled and raised a brow. "Yeah? What kind of chief am I?"

"You're *my* chief."

Epilogue

Gray poked the fire one last time, getting it going nice and hot. Three days before Christmas and it was colder than a witch's tit outside. He sat down on the big red flannel blanket he'd laid in front of the large rock fireplace and stretched out his legs. Wiggling his sock-clad toes, he rested his hands behind his head. *Vacation here I come.* Oh, yeah! This was the life, even if he wasn't going anywhere. Just hanging out on the Broken H was as good a break as a guy could ask for. He'd been re-elected sheriff, Kauffman had been sentenced to a year in the pen, Sherry Ann had gone to live with her aunt and uncle and pretty much everyone who'd criticized Shane for knocking Sherry Ann up had done as predicted and claimed they'd known it couldn't have been true. Life was good.

He had almost everything he needed for the makings of a great nap: fire in the hearth, Christmas music playing quietly in the background, his favorite pair of sweats on. Too bad that he hadn't thought to make himself some hot chocolate with tons of marshmallows before he'd lain down. A nap was always better on a full stomach.

He was just about to fall asleep when the backdoor slammed. Gray rolled his head back, arching his neck a little to see the kitchen doorway.

Shane came stomping into the living room, looking madder than hell. He froze abruptly just inside the doorway between the kitchen and the living room, his surprised but pleased gaze landing on Gray. His expression lightened a little. There was even a hint of a smile. "What are you doing here?"

"I live here."

Shane pulled off his thick wool coat and tossed it onto the couch, then peeled off his gloves and flung them on top of the coat. His hands went to his lean hips. "I mean, what are you doing home?" He glanced at the clock on the mantel. "It's only three o'clock." He moved around to stand at Gray's feet so that Gray didn't have to break his neck to look at him, and grinned, his eyes twinkling. Gray could almost see the last of his bad mood slipping away. "You know, I paid good money to get you re-elected and I know damned well I pay my taxes. So why is my sheriff lounging about in his pajamas in my living room instead of out catching bad guys?"

Gray chuckled. "Your sheriff is on vacation as of two o'clock this afternoon."

"Really?"

"Yup." Gray sat up and patted the floor beside him.

Shane smiled. "I thought your vacation started tomorrow." He dropped down onto the blanket and tugged one boot off, then the other.

Gray shrugged. "I decided to get an early start. Your tax dollars allow me to do that."

Shane laughed. "Oh, they do, do they?"

"Yup, they surely do." He touched the spot next to him again and laid down. "But that's another story. What's got you spitting nails, old man?"

Shane slid all the way onto the flannel blanket and scooted himself around until he was lying next to Gray. "Your daddy." Shane turned on his side, propping himself on his elbow to stare down at Gray.

"Yeah? What'd he do?"

"He willed me half the Broken H."

Gray nodded absently, tracing a finger down Shane's magnificent, albeit covered, chest. The man had way too many clothes on. "Yes, he did, so what?" He raised up so he could unbutton Shane's shirt. *Oh, yeah, there we go...luscious bare skin.*

Shane stilled Gray's hand. "You knew about it?"

Shit! "Uh, yes." He pushed Shane's hand away and unfastened another button.

Shane stopped his hand again, this time clasping it in his own.

"Oh, come on, Chief!" Gray flopped down onto his back. He didn't want to do this now. He was on vacation, damn it!

"Grayson?" Shane arched a brow.

"Shane, does it really matter? Think of it this way. One way or another, you get half of the Broken H when they're gone. You are my partner, my love. What's mine is yours. Did you honestly think I wouldn't put it in your name, too?"

Shane opened his mouth and closed it.

"So, why don't you just let them do this for you? You know they love you. Just say thank you and deal with it. You'll make them happy. With any luck, they won't be gone for quite a long time, anyway." He waited for Shane to argue, but all Shane did was smile.

"Okay."

"Okay?" Gray was skeptical of this seemingly easy acceptance.

Shane nodded firmly. "Okay. I'll go thank them right now." He started to get up.

Gray grabbed his arm. "Wait! Can't you thank them later?"

"I thought you wanted me to let them know I appreciate what they've done." His eyes twinkled.

Gray yanked Shane down and rolled on top of him, straddling the denim-clad hips and started working the shirt again. "Later." Gray freed the last button and pulled the material open. *Oh, yeah! More skin!* His cock perked right up at the sight.

Gray dropped forward onto his hands and caught a nipple in his mouth, rubbing his growing erection against Shane as he did. *Ooh, baby!* He wasn't the only one getting into things. Shane was pretty damn hard himself.

Shane grinned and grabbed his ass, rocking him. "What did you have in mind?"

He raised his head. "A sixty-eight?"

One of those black brows raised.

"You blow me and I'll owe you one." Gray fluttered his eyelashes shamelessly.

Shane guffawed. "Okay, but I want mine right afterward."

"Deal. Let's get on with it, old man." Gray hopped up and tugged his sweat pants down and his T-shirt over his head. He stepped back above Shane and clasped his lover's cock, stroking, stroking, stroking.

"Umm, come here." Shane's gaze raked over him; he licked his lips suggestively.

Gray settled himself over Shane on his knees. He leaned down on one hand and brushed his prick across Shane's lips with the other.

Shane licked around the head, then opened up wide, taking Gray's cock halfway, then sucking strongly.

"Oh, fuck, that feels good." Shane's eyes flicked up to his. There was a glare on his glasses from the fire, but Gray could make out those beautiful big brown eyes just fine. Was there anything finer than the sight of Chief sucking him off?

Shane held his gaze and continued sucking for a moment before he closed his eyes and got down to some serious business, really working Gray's dick. He took hold Gray's ass cheeks, pressing him forward and, with sexy noises, encouraged him to fuck his mouth.

Sensation raced through Gray, making him moan. His lids swept down and he moved his hips, rocking himself into his lover's mouth faster, while still holding the base of Shane's cock. Shane's hand slid down his crease and found Gray's balls, tugging lightly.

Gray tightened, his testicles pulling away from the attention. Saliva ran down his shaft onto Shane's hand. Shane squeezed, adding to Gray's pleasure.

Shane moaned.

He looked down, watching his dick, shiny with spit, sliding in and out of Shane's mouth. There was a drop of something on the lens of Shane's glasses. Sweat or saliva or... "Oh, fuck!" Gray bolted upright, pulling his prick from Shane's mouth and releasing Shane's cock. He pumped his own cock fast, his eyes focusing intensely into Shane's through those lenses. He pushed his shaft down, still pumping vigorously and came...on Shane's glasses. He fell onto one hand, the other one still wrapped around his erection. Oh, damn, that had been incredible. Just the thought of spunking on Shane's glasses had made him come.

Shane wiped a splotch of semen off his cheek with his finger and stuck it in his mouth. Then he froze, finger between his lips and blinked. His eyes crossed for an instant as the white splotches on his glasses apparently registered. Those brown eyes zeroed in on Gray, his lips twitching. "You little shit."

~ * ~

J. L. Langley

J.L. writes M/M erotic romance, among other things, and is fortunate to live with four of the most gorgeous males to walk the earth...ok, so one of those males is canine, but he is quite beautiful for a German Shepherd. J.L. was born and raised in Texas. Which is a good thing considering that Texas is full of cowboys and there is nothing better than a man in a pair of tight Wranglers and a cowboy hat as far as J.L. is concerned.

To contact J.L. Langley, email: langleyjl@gmail.com.

NOW AVAILABLE In Print from Loose Id®

HARD CANDY
Angela Knight, Morgan Hawke and Sheri Gilmore

HOWL
Jet Mykles, Raine Weaver, and Jeigh Lynn

COURTESAN
Louisa Trent

DANGEROUS CRAVINGS
Evangeline Anderson

LEASHED: MORE THAN A BARGAIN
Jet Mykles

THE BROKEN H
J. L. Langley

Publisher's Note: The print titles listed above were previously released in e-book format by Loose Id®.

NEW! Non-fiction from Loose Id®

PASSIONATE INK:
A GUIDE TO WRITING EROTIC ROMANCE
ANGELA KNIGHT

OTHER TITLES Available In Print from Loose Id®

ALPHA

Treva Harte

DINAH'S DARK DESIRE

Mechele Armstrong

HEAVEN SENT: HEAVEN & PURGATORY

Jet Mykles

INTERSTELLAR SERVICE & DISCIPLINE:
VICTORIOUS STAR

Morgan Hawke

RATED: X-MAS

Rachel Bo, Barbara Karmazin & Jet Mykles

THE BITE BEFORE CHRISTMAS

Laura Baumbach, Sedonia Guillone, & Kit Tunstall

THE COMPLETENESS OF CELIA FLYNN

Sedonia Guillone

Publisher's Note: The print titles listed above were previously released in e-book format by Loose Id®.

Ask for These Titles at your FAVORITE BOOKSELLER!

Printed in the United States
97017LV00001B/303/A